A-Level
MUSIC
STUDY GUIDE

David Ventura

Philip Allan Updates
Market Place
Deddington
Oxfordshire
OX15 0SE

Orders
Bookpoint Ltd, 130 Milton Park, Abingdon, Oxfordshire, OX14 4SB
tel: (44) 01235 827720
fax: (44) 01235 400454
e-mail: uk.orders@bookpoint.co.uk
Lines are open 9.00 a.m.–5.00 p.m., Monday to Saturday, with a 24-hour message
answering service. You can also order through the Philip Allan Updates website:
www.philipallan.co.uk

The cover photographs are reproduced courtesy of Ingram, Stefan Kuemmel,
Aleksi Manninen, Sasan Saidi and Daniel Wilson.

All efforts have been made to trace copyright on items used.

All website addresses included in this book are correct at the time of going to
press but may subsequently change.

Design by Juha Sorsa

Printed in Great Britain by CPI Bath

Philip Allan Updates' policy is to use papers that are natural, renewable
and recyclable products and made from wood grown in sustainable forests.
The logging and manufacturing processes are expected to conform to the
environmental regulations of the country of origin.

Contents

Introduction

This book is intended to be a useful resource for students however the A-level music specifications develop in the future. I have avoided reference to any particular examination board, and a variety of approaches have been included in each of the three main areas of this book: performing, composing and appraising. Even if some topic areas are not included in a particular specification, they will prove useful for general musicianship. This convenient categorisation into three subject areas, which has been used in the A-level specifications since 2000, is likely to be reflected in any new specifications, although the subdivision has not been without criticism. Where, for example, does improvisation fit — under performing or composing? Should listening skills be tested as a separate component or assessed within all three units? How should musical history be approached — as musicology, analysis of scores or performing practice? These questions demonstrate the problem of carving up a subject that is essentially a unified art form.

In whatever way music exams are devised in the future, the essential skills of a musician will remain. Specifications will still include performing, composing and appraising. If these titles become more integrated, then that should not be a problem — all we are doing is playing with words. All musical activities require listening skills, whether we are homing in on the sound we make in performance, evaluating the progress of a composition or analysing a Mozart symphony. It is not the prime concern of a student as to whether listening skills are tested separately or as part of an assessment of a performance or composition. These matters can be decided in the exam board offices. What is important is that music students continue to enjoy making music, seeking ways of improving the quality of the musical experience and maintaining the transferable skills that are so useful to society.

The advent of music technology has widened access to the subject for many less formally trained musicians; it has also helped those who have followed a traditional route to create music closer to a professional quality, and has encouraged creativity and motivation. The rapid developments taking place in hardware and software for music-making and the spread of broadband internet provision preclude any useful detailed description of commercially available products. However, I have not been able to resist the inclusion of a few website addresses and a summary of the capabilities of computers at the present time.

This book is not intended to be read straight through. Different sections can be accessed depending on your needs at the time. Some of the hints and tips that may seem obvious to one person will be new ideas for another.

The book is intended to be a combination of reference and hints for students. Teachers may wish to use some sections in a class situation. It will be helpful, for example, if teachers play some of the piano examples to students to reinforce the points made in the text, although some students will be able to do this themselves. The pages could be opened at the charts of music and world history (pages 70–74) if a teacher is trying to contextualise a particular composer or work. The sections on composing techniques only contain one example of each style, but I have tried to draw points from these that are common to the style being studied. Similarly, much of the advice concerning performance could be discussed in greater depth with peripatetic instrumental and vocal coaches, particularly those sections on instrument care and technique.

I would like to thank a number of people for their help and support while writing this book. Colleagues and friends who have made helpful comments include Carol and Joseph Skinner, Peter Fletcher and Rebecca Donaldson. I would also like to thank Philip Allan Updates for having faith in my premise that among the many publications on the market such a volume is needed.

David Ventura, spring 2007

Chapter 1

Performing

Choosing appropriate repertoire

The many excellent conservatories of music established in the UK during the first half of the nineteenth century have trained performers and composers to a high level. Several of these conservatories organise progressive practical examinations at venues throughout the UK, aimed at students learning to play a musical instrument or to sing. These exams provide a structure for lessons given by instrumental teachers, and give students short-term goals and a standard against which to measure their progress. Since the National Curriculum imposed common levels of achievement in all aspects of music education, the standards set by these colleges and conservatories have been measured against a common set of criteria and become roughly comparable. A grade 8 achieved using the Trinity College of Music examinations is roughly equivalent to a grade 8 achieved under the system organised by the Royal Schools of Music (known as the Associated Board). Exam boards provide guidance on the level of difficulty of the music to be performed, by comparing it to these conservatory-based practical tests. For AS, this is grade 5, and for A2 a standard of grade 6 is required.

American grade	Level description	UK equivalent grades	
1	Very easy	1–2	
2	Easy	3–4	
3	Intermediate	4–5	AS
4	Advanced	6–7	A2
5	Difficult	7–8	
6	Professional	8+	

Table 1.1
Comparison of musical grades in the USA and the UK

The pieces of music on the lists provided for these progressive exams are organised into an order of difficulty spanning eight grades, the simplest exam being grade 1. Even with the formation of new exam boards to meet the need for assessment generated by new styles of music-making and popular electronic instruments, this same eight-level system has been adopted. However, equivalent standards have not always been established between institutions. For example, the American band system of grades is generally more difficult, as shown in Table 1.1.

The Yamaha Organ School has grades that work backwards — the professional level is grade 1 and the lowest grade is 9. The Rockschool exams for guitar, bass and drums use the standard UK grade 1–8 system and give opportunities for improvisation within their set pieces. The Associated Board jazz syllabus does the same but at the time of writing only covers clarinet, saxophone, trumpet, trombone and piano from grades 1–5.

When choosing pieces to play for an A-level exam, find out whether the music is on any of the lists of set pieces for the conservatory exams for grade 5 or above. If it is, then it will be of the correct standard. The current syllabuses can be accessed online, and your instrumental teacher will be familiar with pieces that were listed in previous years. Web addresses are as follows:

❖ Associated Board: **www.abrsm.org** and follow the links to exams.

❖ Trinity and Guildhall: **www.trinitycollege.co.uk** and follow the links to music and grade exams.

❖ Rockschool: **www.rockschool.co.uk**; the pieces required are published in their own books for guitar, drums, bass and vocals.

The levels expected by the boards are only guides and it is possible to work around them. For example, the grade 6 expectation at A2 can be an average (assuming each piece has roughly the same duration). Therefore, playing a grade 5 piece and a grade 7 piece will average out at an overall standard of grade 6. It is important to choose music that is well within your technical abilities. Struggling with grade 8 pieces is far less satisfactory than playing grade 5 pieces well. The way A-level examiners mark performance work is different from the Associated Board's method, as a glance at any of the criteria they use reveals.

In addition to the accepted level of difficulty, there are other points to consider when choosing your A-level performance pieces. Do you get nervous on the day? Most people do, and a small amount of nervous energy is often beneficial. See p. 28 for a discussion about strategies to cope with nerves. However, a good starting point is to choose a repertoire that is less likely to raise your anxiety levels.

Here are a few tips on choosing the right music for a recital at A2. Many are also applicable at AS.

1 Choose music that is in some way linked into a cohesive whole. For example:
   a Round the world: music from a variety of countries.
   b American Broadway: songs from the musicals, from George Gershwin and Kurt Weill through to Stephen Sondheim.
   c French flute or saxophone music (perhaps focusing on the early twentieth century when there was an outpouring of good music from this source).
   d A simple historical survey of repertoire, e.g. jazz guitar styles from Django Reinhardt to Martin Taylor.

2 Choose music that demonstrates variety. For example:
   a Different tempos.
   b Different styles, e.g. in a jazz recital some swing, Latin American and a ballad.
   c Different levels of dynamic, e.g. a powerful slow march contrasted with a wistful and delicate character piece.
   d Different textures, e.g. choose one piece intended for unaccompanied performance.

3 Choose music that shows off your particular skills and abilities. For example:
   a Are you a methodical or logical person? If so, a set of variations might suit your playing style.
   b Do you enjoy the small details of your work? A heavily ornamented Baroque piece will suit you.
   c Are you emotionally responsive, an extrovert and willing to take risks? If so, choose from the Romantic repertoire.

4 Mozart's music may appear to be simpler than most, and in respect of the notes this can be true in some cases. However, because of Mozart's understanding of texture the music is often extremely exposed, which can make small slips seem worse than they really are. Such slips are likely to be noticed by your audience and your own confidence can plummet. In addition, Mozart's music demands poise, elegance and a highly developed understanding of balanced phrasing, so unless you feel you have this ability, avoid it. The clarinet concerto, for example, is much more difficult than it seems to be from looking at the score.

5 *Perpetuum mobile* pieces (with flowing semiquaver movement, such as the Toccata by Pietro Domenico Paradies or Fritz Kreisler's arrangement of Nicolò Paganini's *Moto perpetuo* op. 11 no.6 for violin) need special security. Such pieces can trip up the fingers and cause the player to fumble and disrupt the flow.

6　Starting a recital with a piece of *pianissimo* music is difficult. A strong and positive start, with a *forte* or *mezzo-forte* dynamic, will help reduce your nerves, testing both the acoustic of the room and the instrument's responsiveness.

7　If your music is accessible to the average listener then it will go down well in any concert or recital. This will give you a confidence boost after the applause dies down if you are playing more than one piece in a recital. Music that is more challenging for the listener needs careful placing in a programme. For example, the trumpet sonata by Allen Vizzutti is an impressive piece to play but is perhaps better placed towards the end of a group of pieces because of its discordant idiom.

8　The order of the pieces you play is important. Henry T. Fink's maxim is worth remembering: '...first the intellectual, then the emotional, then the sensational' (H. T. Fink (1910) *Success in Music*). A virtuoso 'fireworks' piece is best placed near the end, as it is difficult to choose a piece to follow it.

9　Be careful with the order of keys for each piece. B♭ major followed by A minor will make the second piece sound flat. B♭ major followed by E major in a Baroque recital is uncomfortable because of the tritone relationship between the tonic of each key.

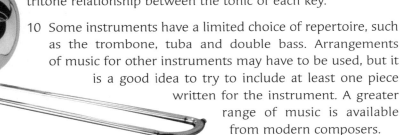

INGRAM

10　Some instruments have a limited choice of repertoire, such as the trombone, tuba and double bass. Arrangements of music for other instruments may have to be used, but it is a good idea to try to include at least one piece written for the instrument. A greater range of music is available from modern composers.

11　If choosing jazz standards for improvisation, try to avoid pieces that are too complicated. A simple starting point will allow you to demonstrate your imagination and creativity in how you develop your solos.

12　Be fair to your accompanist. Choosing music that has a difficult piano part — perhaps derived from an orchestral reduction — will not help you to communicate the music successfully.

13　Rehearse frequently with your accompanist (and your page turner if required), and make sure that you have the opportunity to rehearse in the venue where you are to perform. Pianists and organists should arrange to try out the available instrument in advance. Jazz and rock performers need to have communicated any arrangements well ahead to fellow performers in the band. Short solos from the other members of the band are fine, helping to break up the monotony of a single lead instrument, but these must be restricted in number and length so that *you* are the main performer featured.

14 Find an opportunity to play some or all of your pieces at a concert before your recital to gain valuable experience and confidence.

15 Learn about the background of the composers of your chosen repertoire and prepare a short programme. Exam board requirements differ with regard to mandatory programme notes. However, it is always a good idea to produce notes, in order to focus your own ideas and to provide information for your audience.

16 Take note of the following technical considerations:
   a Pianists with small hands will do best to avoid Rachmaninoff or Brahms. The large chords and hand spans will be tiring to play.
   b If only a small upright piano is available then it is better to avoid a repertoire that focuses on large sonorities. Baroque and Classical pieces are likely to be more effective than late Romantic styles.
   c Brass players should avoid combining pieces that may be tiring on the lip and perhaps also tiring for the listener.
   d Singers need to choose music that is relatively easy to memorise. Their communication with the audience will benefit from plenty of eye contact.
   e Woodwind players need to show the range of playing styles available on their instrument, demonstrating contrast between cantabile lines and agile staccato tonguing. Consider harmonics for tone control and/or dynamic variation. Un-tongued notes are possible for soft beginnings — a 'breath attack' can be used, for example in the solo flute line that opens Debussy's *Prélude à l'après-midi d'un faune*.
   f Double tonguing (*te-ke* or *tuh-kuh*) and triple tonguing (*ta-ka-ta*) is useful for quick passages, as is spiccato for bowed strings.

Practice techniques

You can prepare for your practice session mentally, away from your instrument. In fact, some complete preparatory 'mental rehearsals' will pay dividends when you are learning a piece of music. Study the score and play through the notes in your head so that when you come to your instrument you will be familiar with how the music sounds and will already have considered the technical difficulties. If you find this hard, limit your mental preparation to one aspect of a piece — just the main melodic ideas or a prominent rhythmic motif. Mark the score with ideas, both technical and musical. When you bring this mental image to the instrument you will already have made good progress. Make sure you understand:

❖ the formal structure of the music

❖ the location of the points of climax and rest

❖ why sections might be repeated

- why melodies return later in the music
- where a concluding section or coda begins
- how the music is supposed to sound from a stylistic point of view
- the circumstances in which the piece was first performed

Before you start practising, set yourself some achievable goals for the session. These can be technical or expressive. Technical goals will often contribute to achieving the expressive intentions of the music. Examples of such goals could include:

- reaching a predefined consistent tempo for a difficult passage
- improving the dynamic range of a short Romantic character piece
- strengthening a weak finger
- improving legato, staccato and general articulation
- achieving a sense of natural swing in a jazz solo
- identifying points to breathe and adjusting phrasing

You should have a plan before beginning a practice session. There are many possibilities, depending on the instrument and the music to be practised. However, there is nothing wrong with following unexpected developments and postponing the stated goal to a follow-up session. This can be a more exciting approach, but if you consistently avoid the stated goals you might need to review them. It may help to have shorter sessions in order to concentrate on specific goals.

Warm up away from your instrument. You wouldn't dream of running a 100-metre sprint without first warming up your muscles. Neither should you expect your body to cope with the considerable demands put upon it by performing music without getting it ready physically. First, stretch your arms and move your neck around, rotate your arms and elbows, shake your wrists and bend your knees. Take some slow, deep breaths. Slow controlled movements of the hands and fingers are valuable.

Check your posture — if you are uncomfortable, there is probably something wrong. If there is a mirror in the room, study your reflection to see if you are standing in an exaggerated or awkward position. Your teacher will advise you on the best way to hold your instrument, but here are a few tips:

1 **Keyboard players:** adjust your stool so that your back is relatively straight and you are not too far away from the keyboard. Elbows should be bent. If the stool is too low, you will find playing hard work, and loud passages will be difficult to create with just fingers and wrists. If it is too high, there is a danger that the music will lose many of the subtleties that rely on sensitive finger control. Sit towards the front of the stool and keep your wrists loose. For more advice visit http://pianoeducation.org/pnotmi1.html and www.balancedpianist.com/index.htm.

2   **Violinists:** do not hunch up your left shoulder, and make sure that your shoulder rest is correctly fitted. You should also avoid locking the left hand and holding the bow with too strong a grip. Don't raise the left hand fingers too high, especially in fast passages.

3   **Cellists:** take care to support your back and keep your body relaxed.

4   **Classical guitarists:** avoid resting your inner arm against the instrument. Shoulders should be level and your head central. Keep relaxed and have breaks to stretch your body. Rock guitarists should ensure that they have a wide strip to support the axe.

5   **Woodwind players:** ensure sound holes are completely covered by the finger pads. Flute players, in particular, have to play their instrument with an unnatural body position and it is important to take frequent breaks. You can help the free movement of your fingers by wedging the instrument between your hands and chin rather than supporting it with the left thumb. Saxophone players should push the instrument away from their body rather than letting it hang on the side.

6   **Brass players:** study your embouchure to make sure you are not developing a drift with your mouthpiece away from the centre of your lips. Hold the instrument up to transmit the sound, making sure the music stand is adjusted appropriately.

7   Hand position is also important, as most instruments use fingering to produce different pitches. Keyboard players' hands must avoid falling over towards the little fingers and should cradle an imaginary tennis ball.

8   **Singers:** keep your head up and your shoulders relaxed. Visit **www.vocalist. org.uk**, for advice on posture, breathing and many vocal techniques.

You need to adopt an analytical approach to practice in order to make progress and be able to perform your pieces with a high level of security. It is important to bear in mind that when you are practising you should *really* be practising and not just performing to parents and friends in the next room. Playing through pieces from start to finish can help develop an overview of how your pieces will work as part of a programme, but doing this repeatedly is not helpful.

Playing through a piece of music, slowing down for a difficult section and then speeding up again is not recommended unless it is a

deliberate stylistic consideration such as rubato in a Chopin arabesque. You need to identify which phrases or motifs might be causing a disruption in fluency. You can then focus on the required technical control by working on the phrase at a slower pace. If there is a passage where you always seem to slip up but are finding it difficult to identify the actual problem, then **group practice** is a good approach. This involves shifting the groupings of notes so that the problems reveal themselves. The method is illustrated below by the right hand part of a Bach two-part invention:

Group practice for two-part invention no.11

J. S. Bach BWV782

A similar approach can also be used for practising the following short phrase, which is part of the slow movement of Weber's first clarinet concerto:

Group practice for clarinet concerto phrase

C. M. von Weber

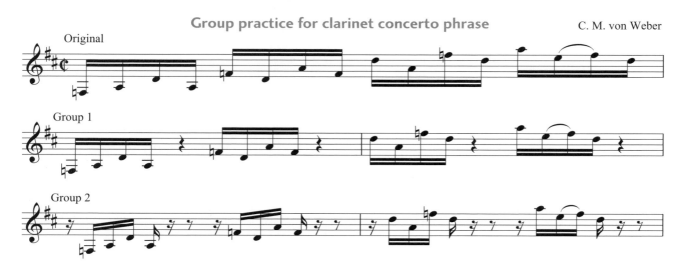

Group 3

Group 4

The problem is often a particular technical difficulty, such as widespread hands on the piano or rapid tonguing on the recorder. Using written studies that feature such techniques is helpful and can provide you with a welcome diversion from the music you are studying. Large compendia of studies are available that cover almost the whole range of playing techniques, such as the Arban cornet tutor. Some of these can be a little dry, but there are plenty of interesting pieces that are more than just technical exercises. You need to be sure that the study you have chosen concentrates on the difficulty you are facing. Examples of appropriate studies are given below. The focus in the first example is on the melody played by the left hand thumb in the nocturne by John Field. The study by Stephen Heller is not too difficult and allows extra practice for this technique.

Nocturne no. 7

John Field

Study no. 16

Stephen Heller, op. 45

The performance of the large leaps in Mozart's flute concerto (below) can be improved by practising Boehm's Study.

Concerto in D major for Flute

W. A. Mozart, к314

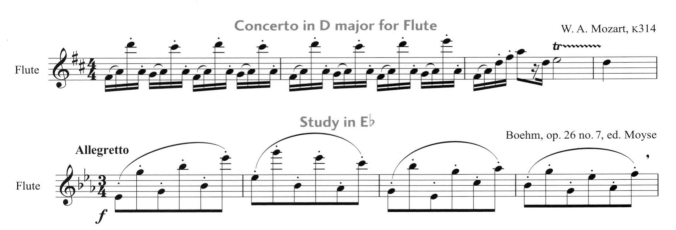

Over-practising a particular technique can damage tendons in the hand or muscles around the mouth. If there is any pain involved in such repetitive exercises you should stop, relax and work on another aspect of the piece.

Relaxation techniques are dealt with later in this chapter (see page 28). However, there are some useful ways of relaxing your muscles during practice. Pianists can practise hands separately, with and without pedalling and with the unused arm hanging down loosely at their side. Woodwind players might try playing the rhythm only, without moving their fingers, and brass players can sing the music while fingering the valves or moving the slide. Singers can try speaking the words in rhythm and string players might play the rhythm of the music using just the bow on the correct string but relaxing the other hand.

For singers and wind players, breathing exercises are critical. Good breath control is integral to how the musical phrases can be delivered and is also an important contributor to good intonation. Breathing exercises can include the following:

❖ Stand up straight but in a relaxed posture, with your arms by your side. Breathe in slowly while raising your arms out straight, until they are over your head, with the backs of your hands facing out. Hold for a few seconds, then slowly lower your arms while breathing out. Repeat five times.

❖ Place one hand on your chest and one on your stomach just above your navel. Relax and breathe slowly in and out. The hand on your stomach should rise and fall and the one on your chest stay still. This exercise can also be carried out lying down.

❖ Pant slowly in time to a slow pulse of four in a bar, then move to panting in quavers and semiquavers when you have warmed up.

Wind players can purchase a chromatic tuner. You can use this to tune your instrument to a mid-range, reliable note (saxophones should avoid C♯), then play an octave higher and observe whether the tuner is still registering the note as in tune. Play at the same volume if possible. Loud notes can sound flat on a clarinet and sharp on a flute.

Another idea is to try playing with your eyes closed. For instruments such as keyboards and percussion this will help to develop a 'mental map' of the exact location of the keys or playing surfaces. Pianists can also try crossing their hands and playing the top part two octaves down and the lower line two octaves up. This approach is dependent on the music itself but works particularly well with Bach or Mozart.

Practising with a metronome can help with problems of timing and can reveal an incorrect rhythm or inappropriate tempo change. There are also CDs of accompaniments available commercially (see **www.piano-accompaniments.com**). These techniques must be used with caution to avoid forcing your performance into a straightjacket.

Performing with a sense of history

Performing practice is a discipline of study that is relatively recent. Research in this area has grown since the late 1960s, with David Munrow and Christopher Hogwood and their recordings of Medieval and Renaissance music. In more recent years, recordings that use original instruments designed for performance

in Classical and Romantic orchestras have become popular. These recordings give the listener an insight into how the music was intended to sound.

Performing practice concentrates on the implementation of the way music of the past is thought to have been played, which in turn was influenced by the social circumstances and musical instrument technology of the time. The intentions of the composer should be taken into account if the meaning of the music is to be communicated successfully. Similarly, the expectations of the original audience are a factor in the equation, and worth researching and thinking about.

In the absence of recordings, information can be derived from reports of concerts in letters and newspapers, together with learned treatises on playing techniques. In many cases you will be able to rely on modern editors, who have taken such research into account when publishing their scores. However, the correct interpretation of the music is not always evident from the score. In addition, some A-level exam boards ask for a personal evaluation of your own performance, so it is useful to have some understanding of performing practice. Playing the music accurately according to the printed page is not the whole story, although of course a good proportion of examination mark schemes credit this aspect.

The Baroque period (1600–1750)

The music of the Baroque rejoiced in its sense of musical direction, as the tonal system became established and the technology of instrument manufacture improved. Grandiose flourishes, expressive ornamentation, learned counter-point and the direct communication required of opera mixed to form the rich Baroque style. The printing presses had developed from the days of William Byrd and they used lithograph techniques to produce large quantities of high quality printed music. However, divergences from the original manuscripts were already appearing in performances. In fact, in some styles of music — notably the French clavecin repertoire — artistic interpretation became of equal importance to the realisation of the printed score. The artist would freely embellish the music with ornaments.

Another characteristic of French music at the time, particularly in dance music, was the use of *notes inégales*. Literally 'unequal notes', this meant that performers would play running quavers as a long note followed by a short one, in much the same way as jazz players now produce swung rhythms. The music of Henry Purcell and John Blow in England was influenced by the French style (Charles II had spent his youth in Paris and brought back a preference for French mannerisms).

Baroque ornamentation is a huge subject, beyond the scope of this book. Some good modern editions provide prefaces with explanations of the grace notes used in the music. There are a few agreed common traits, however, including the principle that appoggiaturas, trills, mordents and turns must begin *on* the beat, as set out on p. 13.

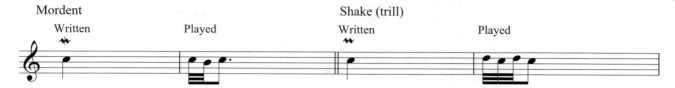

(Note: the sign for the mordent became the sign for inverted mordent in the nineteenth century and that for the shake became the standard mordent. In Baroque music, trills and shakes begin on the upper note.)

The complex subject of ornamentation is set out clearly at: **www.dolmetsch. com/musictheory23.htm**

The aristocratic viol consort was superseded during the first half of the seventeenth century by the violin family, which became the most important ensemble instruments of the Baroque period. Their expressive yet direct sound quality and improvements in manufacture by violin makers made their rise a rapid one. Cremona, in northern Italy, was the home of two important makers — Nicolò Amati (1596–1684) and Antonio Stradiveri (1644–1737) — whose instruments fetch huge sums of money in auctions today. However, there was a divergence in playing styles across Europe. A common rule was to play with a down bow at the start of each bar, but in triple time this was achieved differently, as set out below:

Players would hold the bow at varying points along its wooden shaft to achieve delicate nuances. Marks of expression were not as copiously notated as in modern music and the performer was expected to add these. Vibrato was rarely used except as a special effect. The idiosyncratic music of Heinrich von Biber was full of special effects, including tremulando (rapidly repeating a note), scordatura (changing the tuning) and col legno (using the wood of the bow instead of the hair). The viola and cello used fewer expressive ornaments than the violin.

The flute and oboe were the most important wind instruments at this time, although the trumpet and bassoon featured in orchestral music. The recorder suffered the same fate as the viol, as its more intimate sound was generally less useful to dramatic composers. (Notable exceptions were when a pastoral scene or bird impressions were required on stage.) The flute was made of wood and had a sound that was more mellow than its modern equivalent. All Baroque woodwind instruments created a softer sound than we are accustomed to today. The writing would often imitate vocal techniques and tonguing would reflect this. Trumpet music was normally associated with praise and majesty or war-like scenes.

There was a great variety of styles in vocal music for church, chamber and theatre. For example:

- ❖ Different tone colours were used across the various vocal ranges (modern singers try to disguise these).
- ❖ High notes sung by the 'head' voice were soft and light and the low 'chest' voice had more volume.
- ❖ Sudden dynamic changes were frowned upon.
- ❖ Long notes were normally given crescendos or diminuendos, to add interest and shape.
- ❖ Notes were clearly articulated and semi-staccato, except in slow adagios.

It is worth comparing recordings of Baroque music by modern ensembles with older recordings by respected artists. For example, compare John Eliot Gardiner with Otto Klemperer, the Taverner Consort with David Willcocks or Trevor Pinnock with Raymond Leppard. The tempo of the music, the resources used and the general style is likely to be very different.

The Classical period (1750–1800)

In the Classical period the taste was for less heavily decorated and complex music. The emphasis was on elegance and style. Note lengths were generally given less than their full value until the last decade of the eighteenth century, when Muzio Clementi stated a preference for full values and detached playing symbols became important. Ornamentation tended to be indicated in the score rather than improvised. It wasn't until the nineteenth century that it became standard for trills to begin on the written note, rather than the note above.

The piano emerged as the dominant concerto instrument and it also featured in solo sonatas and chamber music. It gradually superseded the harp-sichord, as it was able to express individual note dynamics. Haydn's early keyboard works were written for harpsichord, but later the piano became his preferred choice.

There were two main types of piano — Viennese and English/French — and these were different in character. The Viennese piano was clear and light, with an immediate action — the hammer was connected directly to the key, which travelled only a short distance to its key bed, and therefore the music could be given detailed articulation through touch. The sustain pedal (lifting the dampers) was used rarely and only for sections with the same harmony, and it was operated by a knee lever. Thus in the music of Mozart we find detailed annotations of slurring and staccato, because these could be achieved success-fully with the fingers. It is important for a modern performer to render these as accurately as possible, bearing in mind that a modern piano's heavier tone will not achieve the historical sound. It is enough, however, to realise the importance of these markings.

*Broadwood's piano
factory, Horseferry
Road, London, 1842*

The Broadwood pianos from London and later the Eckhardts from Paris had a different sound from the Viennese piano. These piano makers concentrated on a sound that had a longer, richer sustaining tone and came with pedals operated by the feet, as in the modern instrument. Beethoven was given one of these pianos and he greatly admired it, although it is said he still preferred his old Viennese one. His music generally expects more use of the sustain pedal, but his fondness for sudden sforzandos is better delivered on a Viennese instrument.

Which instrument was the Classical piano music you are playing originally written for? You can assume the Viennese piano for Haydn, Mozart and Beethoven and the English for Field and Clementi. If in doubt, study the music and decide whether it demands a light and clear sound or a sustained and full one. The following two extracts reflect the different approaches, and were composed within a few years of each other.

Sonata in F

W. A. Mozart, K332, mvt 2

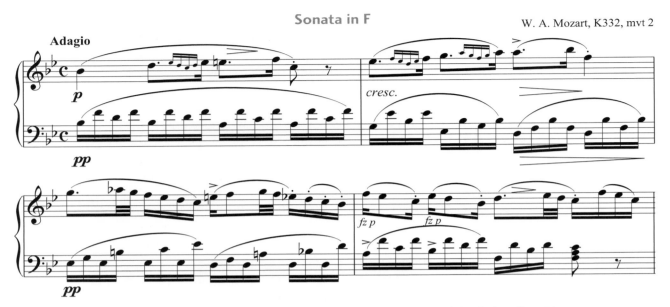

Note the elegant melody, the detailed articulation and the light Alberti bass.

Piano Sonata in F♯ minor

M. Clementi op. 25, no. 5 mvt 2

Note the bass pedal harmony, the sad, long melody and phrasing.

Allowances need to be made when playing on a modern piano, especially a grand. The power of this instrument is more than would have been available in the eighteenth century. Chords in the bass and tenor ranges can sound muddy and tone development is relatively slow. Both types of Classical piano produce a clearer sound than the modern concert grand. Mozart's music demands very little pedalling, unlike the music of Beethoven.

Stringed instruments developed extra volume and brilliance during this time. The most important development was the modern bow, perfected by François Tourte. It was championed by the violin virtuoso Giovanni Battista Viotti, who came to Paris from Italy in 1782 and played with a powerful tone and great energy, balanced with the expressive playing characteristic of the old convex bows. When fingering your music you should remember that in Classical music, phrasing is paramount. It is not recommended that you change left-hand positions mid-phrase — an extension of the little finger may be more appropriate if needed. Open strings are to be avoided, as they are also likely to disrupt a consistent tone, and harmonics are definitely out.

Vibrato was more commonly used during the Classical era than in the Baroque, but it was still reserved for long notes. The *mezza di voce* ('placing of the voice') was applied to long notes: a crescendo followed by a diminuendo. Quicker notes required short bow strokes. Dotted notes were still likely to be lengthened, especially in France.

Wind instruments also changed during this time. The clarinet family had superseded the chalumeau but some of the trills were unavailable and a variety of clarinet pitches were used (A, B♭, B, C and D were the most common). The flute used a finger vibrato, but as the century progressed this was replaced by vibrato produced by breath; this technique was restricted to slow movements. Horns were still without valves, but music in the lower register was written and the full scale was accessed using hand-stopping. This technique produced some notes that were muffled in tone. In Vienna, Anton Weidinger invented a keyed trumpet that was used for the two famous concertos by Haydn and Johann Nepomuk Hummel. It has a softer tone than the modern valve trumpet.

Singers were expected to embellish the melodic line, especially in repeated sections. Some modern editions suggest ornaments by adding small notes to the score. If you are worried that exam boards will penalise you for performing music that has too many repeats (with the accusation of not having prepared enough music), then ensure that the repeats contain appropriate ornamentation. Certain decorations were mandatory, such as an appoggiatura at an imperfect cadence. Again, good editions should have these written out for you. Short cadenzas should be employed when there is a pause, as seen in this example:

Will Crutchfield, in his useful chapter on voices in the New Grove Handbook *Performance Practice* (1989), identified four characteristics of the Italian vocal style (the predominant style adopted by most of Western Europe at that time) from the Classical period:

1 the unification of the chest and head voice so that a smooth transition between the two occurs

2 the use of the crescendo and diminuendo on long notes (*mezza di voce*)

3 a smooth legato between notes (*portamento di voce*)

4 the mastery of a core group of ornamental devices, including:
   a appoggiatura
   b trill
   c gruppetto (a turn, or a trill with a turn at the end)
   d volata (a series of quick notes)

Vibrato was still not the norm but was reserved as special decoration.

The Romantic period (1800–1900)

In the Romantic period, the piano became the most important instrument. Its development into a much larger and more powerful model, with an extended range, went hand-in-hand with the Romantic goals of composers. Schubert and Schumann in Vienna still favoured the Viennese pianos. These had become larger and more powerful but retained their clarity of sound. Their lack of sustaining power was offset by the fact that performance spaces in those days were generally more reverberant.

A Pleyel grand piano dating from 1837

Schumann's idiomatic piano textures make use of the sustaining pedal to help with legato octaves and resonance. The French Pleyel piano was popular in Paris and was used by Chopin. He valued the combination of the sustained sound of the English design with the clarity of the straight stringing. Chopin's music is full of the exploitation of sonorities and the sympathetic vibrations of strings created from overtones generated by the main notes. It is important to be aware of these effects when performing his music. Below is an example of a particularly colouristic passage from Chopin's *Berceuse*, a gentle, rocking lullaby. It would have been extremely effective on the silvery tones of the Pleyel piano.

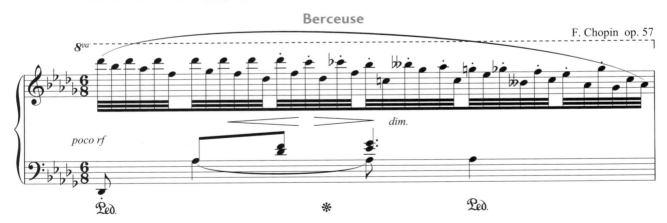

Berceuse

F. Chopin op. 57

Chopin was famous not only for his virtuoso technique but also as being a 'poet of the piano', specialising in the use of expressive rubato. All Romantic music makes use of rubato to a greater or lesser extent. The term translates as 'robbed', and refers to the idea of stolen time, when performers would speed up and then 'repay' their theft by slowing down again. Arabesques (clusters of grace notes) demand a deceleration of the tempo to make them effective, and the phrasing of a cantabile melody would expect to be made demonstrably clear by employing rubato. The overall tempo of the music is often easier to determine by this time, as composers would sometimes indicate precise speeds using J. N. Maelzel's metronome, which began commercial manufacture in 1816.

The large Erard pianos developed for Liszt's prodigious skill are similar to the modern grand piano. Liszt was famous for his orchestral transcriptions, and the technique of imitating orchestral sonorities in piano compositions had been a favourite device of composers since the time of Beethoven (see passages of the development section of the 'Waldstein' Sonata, op. 53, where there are antiphonal woodwind motifs, or more explicitly in the Sonata op. 81a 'Les adieux', with its farewell French horns). The big Steinway concert grands produced music of tremendous power, but it was not until the start of the twentieth century — with composers such as Rachmaninoff — that these became the pianos of choice.

Ludwig van Beethoven, 1804

Other instruments

❖ **Stringed** instruments gained higher tension strings (although the top two were still made from gut and the lower two metal-wound). Hand shift positions were much more frequent (semitone shifts were used in legato passages, with repeated sequences using the same fingerings). Special effects were thoroughly explored by Nicolò Paganini, the great Italian touring virtuoso violinist — especially left-hand pizzicato and harmonics.

❖ The design of the **flute** dates back to Boehm's design of 1847, and other woodwind instruments adopted Boehm fingering systems during the following decade. This flute produced a more powerful sound than the old wooden and conical bore models. The new flute would have been the preferred model for large orchestral works, while the more mellow sounds of older designs were still used for chamber music.

❖ By the nineteenth century the **clarinet** was a much more capable instrument. Iwan Müller, a clarinet designer living in Paris, advocated practising using violin music and becoming fluent in all keys. He also played with the reed below the mouthpiece, which enabled the clarinet to play *pianissimo*. (It was common to play the clarinet with the reed uppermost, which gave it a harsher sound.)

❖ Improvements in **bassoon** design were taking place in an attempt to counter problems with tone, intonation and trills. The modern instrument has a quality of sound far superior to the nineteenth-century models.

❖ Although valve **horns** were available by this time, composers generally preferred the sonority of natural horns. A natural horn depended on the harmonics produced by the vibrating air from the player's lips. Chromatic notes were obtained by adding extra tubing (crooks) or by shortening the air column with the hand in the bell. Valve horns had extra tubing attached, which was accessed by fingers operating the valves. Many orchestras employed two natural horn players and two valve horn players to cover all necessities.

❖ Valved **trumpets** dominated in the second half of the nineteenth century, while in Paris the natural trumpet was complemented by the valved cornet, for example in Hector Berlioz's *Symphonie Fantastique*.

❖ Slide **trombone** pedal notes were popular in music of the time, as was the valve trombone in the orchestra, alongside the recently invented ophicleide. Trills and fast chromatic scales were possible on the valve trombone and ophicleide.

❖ For the **voice**, the Italian bel canto singing style was dominant in the first half of the century, exemplified by the works of Rossini, Bellini and Donizetti. The sweet tone and even legato of this style was copied throughout Europe.

The Romantic song cycle was a form of dramatic storytelling that was popular in chamber salons. The importance of the piano accompaniment in lieder by Schubert, Schumann and Brahms cannot be underestimated, contributing to a form of music that is almost a duet between piano and voice. If you are going to perform lieder you must remember that your accompanist is an equal partner, and you should study the piano part to work out its relationship to the vocal line.

French opera was grandiose, influenced by Italian techniques and also by Wagner's ideas of the drama being paramount. Singers needed to project above the growing orchestral forces, which meant that the main consideration for singers was to develop more vocal power. As opera became less fragmented into formal structures such as the aria, there were fewer opportunities for singers to improvise and embellish the music. Exceptions to this trend were the expressive cantabile andantes and the faster caballetas, which included embellished repeats and cadenzas full of scales and turns (although these were often written out). For repeats, the doubling of the vocal line in the orchestra was sometimes omitted to allow the singer more freedom. The performance of many modern popular ballads that utilise a simplified piano accompaniment would be much improved if accompanists adopted this approach.

The twentieth century to the present

There continued to be divergences of performance style during the twentieth century, in spite of the advent of recording technology and improved transport and communications. The first half of the century favoured the gradual adoption of a continuous vibrato for singers and strings, but not for wind (with the exception of the French flute school, with its bright tone and flexible phrasing). String players used the technique of portamento (sliding between notes). Piano players such as Rachmaninoff would allow a tenuto more time but shorten the following note to maintain a steady pulse.

While the early part of the twentieth century was characterised by differing methods of interpretation, the second half tended towards evenness and a more international language developed. Local idiosyncrasies were ironed out as performers travelled around the world. Commercial considerations (which had always influenced composers and performers) came to the fore in the fields of popular music and jazz.

Jazz, rock and blues, traditional folk music and the myriad of popular styles that developed in the New World highlighted the inadequacy of the written notation system that had developed in Europe from the Middle Ages. The living art of music demands the capability of performers to make minute adjustments to pitch, rhythm, timbre and sound level as the music progresses, and human expression is much more subtle than written notes can represent. This has always been the case, but the problem was exacerbated by the fact that these styles had an unprecedented emphasis on rhythmic vitality and microtonal inflections, as well as a greatly increased range of dynamics.

The music below is a notated version of Eddie 'Lockjaw' Davis's tenor sax solo from 'Splanky' by Neal Hefti — a track from *The Atomic Mr Basie* by the Count Basie Big Band. The transcription misses out on the many musical nuances the soloist plays, some of which are listed below the score. There are various signs and symbols for tenuto, accent and pitch bend, but even if these were used they would only go part of the way towards representing the sound, and would certainly fail to capture the heart or the 'feel' of the delivery.

Splanky

Tenor sax solo as improvised by Eddie 'Lockjaw' Davis

Bar 1: accent on the G♭

Bar 2: accented G♭ with smear

Bar 3: accented swell halfway through the E♭ on beat 3

Bar 4: accents on F and D♭ . A weaker accent on the A♭

Bar 5: pitch bend/slur up on a D♭

Bar 6: G♭ delayed with slight vibrato

Bar 7: first four notes sluggish for a laid-back feel

Bar 8: E♮ slurred up in pitch slightly

Bar 9: second G extremely quiet — hardly played

Bar 10: first note 'squeezed' out

All quavers have a swing feel:

Most notes are slurred except for the tongued accented notes. You should listen carefully to the whole tenor sax solo on this track as a good example of jazz swing.

This piece demonstrates the problem with transcriptions. It is better to learn the music of the jazz masters by listening to recordings and reproducing it by ear, although this kind of detailed written analysis can be useful. The original tracks would have been improvised and most exam boards have a separate set of criteria to accredit improvisation.

Improvisation

To produce a good improvisation you need to have control of your instrument's technical capabilities so that your ideas can be realised by your fingers. It is a good idea to practise a variety of scales — not just the usual major and minor ones but modal, pentatonic and Eastern scales, starting on every note of the chromatic scale. In jazz and rock the relationship to the chord progressions in the music is important. Although an obsession with following them can lead to rather stilted improvisations, chord progressions can be a useful starting point to build up confidence in improvising, by adding passing and auxiliary notes to broken chord patterns:

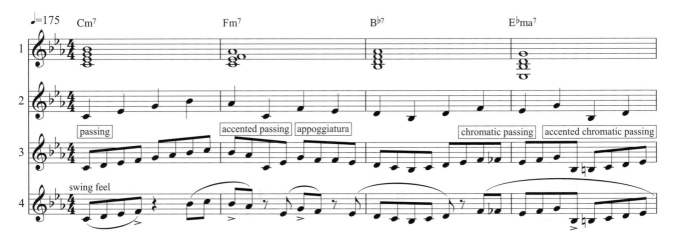

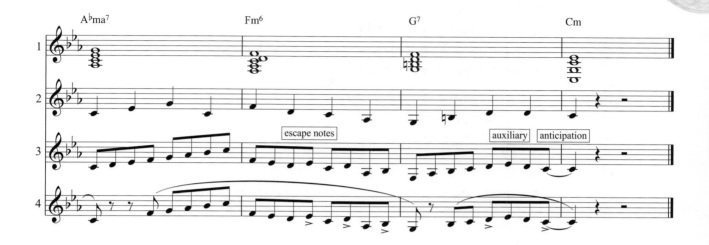

Line 1: given chord progression

Line 2: notes derived from chords

Line 3: with added 'inessential' notes

Line 4: an attempt to make this exercise more 'jazzy' by use of inserted rests, accents and phrase marks

The chords supplied in this example are simple diatonic ones. Therefore, the style of jazz is more likely to emulate the 1930s and 1940s rather than the later years, when bebop players explored harmonies that were much more chromatic. Their improvisations included extended chords such as dominant 9ths, 11ths and 13ths, and chromatically altered chords.

An example is given below, using the dominant chord. Here, the 3rd and 7th remain unaltered whereas the extensions are chromatically shifted:

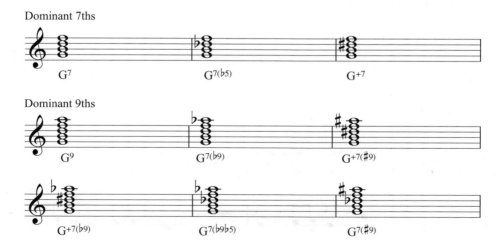

Dominant 11ths

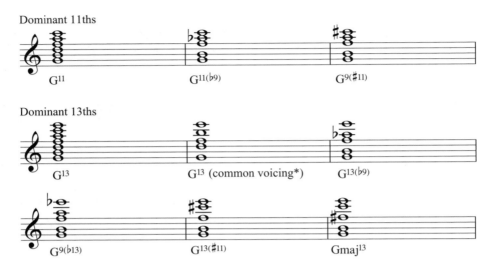

G^{11}　　　　$G^{11(\flat9)}$　　　　$G^{9(\sharp11)}$

Dominant 13ths

G^{13}　　　G^{13} (common voicing*)　　　$G^{13(\flat9)}$

$G^{9(\flat13)}$　　　　$G^{13(\sharp11)}$　　　　$Gmaj^{13}$

* Often composers do not use all the available notes. This is a common distribution of notes (voicing) for G^{13}.

(Note: for chords with large numbers of notes, it is usual to omit some of the less defining notes, such as the 5th and the 11th in a 13th chord.)

Although careful consideration has to be given to harmony, much improvisation is essentially linear, and for this reason familiarity with some of the less common scales is a good idea. Rock guitarists use the blues pentatonic scale as it lies comfortably under the fingers, but they should not be limited to this. The overall shape of the improvisation also needs to be considered: is there variety in the phrase lengths and do they build up towards a climax, perhaps by increasing in length? Although concentration is required for improvisation, it is best to adopt a free, unbuttoned approach. If you enjoy your playing the audience will too.

A recital for A-level music can feature a substantial amount of improvisation. The charts that are used for a jazz improvisation, or the stimulus that is the inspiration for a freestyle soundscape, must be provided for the assessment. This enables the examiner to calculate the degree of technical control you have of your instrument and the amount of inventiveness and thematic transformation you have used.

You may need a backing group, but you must make sure you take the lead and that improvisations by other group members are kept to a minimum. Examiners use different marking criteria when a recital is largely improvised.

One way to escape from the seemingly restrictive techniques mentioned so far is to concentrate on variety in rhythm. Try inventing an interesting solo based on one repeated note only — perhaps in a Latin American style, as demonstrated in Antônio Carlos Jobim's *One Note Samba*. Here is an example of taking a phrase of repeated notes further in that style:

One Note Rhumba

Much can be achieved with rhythmic inventiveness, not only in the jazz idiom but also in the rock guitar solo. Often this style's impact relies on rapidly repeated figuration, bending of pitch, harmonics and sound processing. The use of asymmetrical phrase lengths, long held notes with developing vibrato and pitch bends, hammer-ons and pull-offs, harmonics and slides all add to the variety and interest for the listener. It is important that you identify the techniques you may have used in personal evaluations and write-ups of your performance. Make the examiners aware of your performing skills.

Aspects of style: a summary

Be aware of these aspects of style when preparing music from the following historical periods:

1 Baroque
  a ornamentation and decoration
  b ceremonial function or dance forms
  c contrapuntal lines
  d continuo support of the harmonic progression

2 Classical
  a elegance and poise
  b the importance of form and structure
  c balanced phrases and cadences
  d *style galant* — designed to be entertaining and graceful
  e influence of opera
  f balance between free expression and discipline

3 Romantic
  a individualism and personal feeling
  b national character
  c grandiose statements or miniature pictures
  d extrovert playing, showmanship and impulsiveness
  e playing around with the tempo: rubato
  f extremes of an instrument's normal capabilities

g the piano imitating orchestral sounds and textures

h influence of the other arts, especially literature

4 Twentieth century to the present
a precision
b mathematical relationships
c extending beyond the instrument's normal capabilities
d experiments and challenges
e shock, novelty, sarcasm and irony
f world music influences

5 Jazz
a swing and rhythmic freedom
b syncopation and accent
c playing around with intonation: blue notes etc.
d experimentation and exploration

6 Rock
a groove (i.e. adjusting the rhythm to fit the feel of the music)
b forward movement
c rhythmic emphasis
d lead lines featuring wide dynamic range, with backing sounds often employing compression
e exploring timbre and using electronic effects as an integral part of the music
f playing around with intonation: blue notes etc.
g the importance of lyrics

7 Folk
a openness — clarity of textures and instrumentation
b clarity of the message
c sense of tradition
d acoustics

These characteristics are based on musical stereotypes and do not encompass all considerations when playing music of a particular period. See if you can add to the lists from researching the music you are going to perform.

Tips for the recital

1 Photocopy pages to help with any difficult page turns (this is legal under the British Code of Practice).

2 Consider the aims of the composer. What does the music try to portray? Translate any titles or performance indications.

3 Wear comfortable clothing and warm up well by playing scales and exercises.

4   Ensure you have sufficient light in order to see the music clearly.

5   Discuss your recital with your instrumental teacher or vocal coach and find out well in advance the requirements of the exam board. Peripatetic teachers often complain that the repertoire is chosen too late to do it justice.

6   Singers should attempt to memorise their music so that they can make frequent eye contact with the audience — an important part of communicating the music.

7   Stand slightly to the side of your music stand so that the audience can see you clearly. You will also need to be able to see your accompanist.

Considerations for specific instruments

❖ **Strings:** ensure you have spare strings, a well-haired bow and spare rosin. Make sure your bridge and soundpost are adjusted correctly. Classical guitarists need to think about the issue of projection of sound in a large room. You could consider some subtle sound reinforcement with a condenser microphone (don't be tempted to amplify the sound totally, as this will change the warm acoustic sound of a Spanish guitar). Rock guitarists need to be confident that all their leads are in good condition and batteries for foot pedal processors are new.

❖ **Woodwind:** examine all your springs and pads carefully. Tune with an electronic tuner at different octaves — it is a common fault that students tune a note in mid-register and then blow out of tune in a performance, particularly in the high register. Flautists should use a cleaning rod to adjust the headjoint. Reed instrument players must carry a few spare reeds that have been played in and produce a good sound. Clarinet and saxophone players should choose a reed appropriate to the sound and style of music they are playing — hard reeds are more appropriate for a big jazz sound. Make sure the ligature and reed lay is adjusted correctly.

❖ **Brass:** don't change you mouthpiece at the last minute. Make a careful examination of the condition of your valves or slide — you don't want them sticking halfway through a difficult passage. Check there is no leakage at the spit valve, as this will spoil your tone. Tune carefully, considering the individual valves, by playing a range of chromatic notes. Warm up by playing long notes and lip slurs.

❖ **Piano:** practise on the recital piano in advance so that you can get used to its sound and the weight of the keys. If you have a choice of instruments,

Tips for the recital

choose light weighted keys for jazz. Make sure the pedals don't squeak, and if you have a middle pedal (selective sustain) make sure you can control it properly. You should also practise with the lid raised. The sound will be noticeably different.

Minimising performance anxiety

First, you need to remember that a certain amount of anxiety can be useful in providing the adrenalin required for an exciting performance. However, if you are so anxious that your performance may not represent your natural ability, there are a number of strategies to consider. The approaches to this problem can be divided into physical and emotional methods.

Physical methods

- ❖ Control your diet: avoid caffeine and other stimulants on the day, but don't starve yourself.
- ❖ Exercise: keep fit so that your body can cope with the demands made on it during a performance.
- ❖ Relaxation techniques: breathe deeply or progressively relax your muscles with alternate tension and release.
- ❖ Ensure the music you are about to play is well within your range of ability.

Emotional methods

- ❖ Get used to performing in front of an audience.
- ❖ Carry out 'mental rehearsals'.
- ❖ Be confident that the music is thoroughly prepared.
- ❖ Act calmly immediately before you start, so that you do not become pre-occupied with anxiety.
- ❖ Think positively: don't worry if you make a few minor errors. It is the overall effect that counts. The audience will be on your side and will *want* to enjoy the event.
- ❖ Become totally involved with the music, while retaining an awareness of the audience.

Ensemble performance

Working in groups is a requirement of all the examination boards. This recognises the immense benefits that musical ensembles can bring to the developing musician. Naturally, the standard large ensembles exclude some instruments, but it should be possible to work around this where necessary. For example, a rock guitar player will benefit from singing in a choir: this improves sight-reading and aural awareness, and demonstrates a commitment to musical progress. Similarly, the classical violinist who has learned to play by working through prescribed notated scores will gain enormously from participation in small, improvised jazz or folk ensembles, although this does not need to be part of the formal assessment. For the purposes of this section, ensemble work can be divided into three types: the directed ensemble, the self-directed ensemble and original music with jazz and rock bands.

The directed ensemble

This includes orchestras, choirs and bands, as well as larger groups that need a director or conductor. Most schools have such activities available, and smaller schools may have links to county organisations. Ensure that you make use of the opportunities on offer. The benefits can include:

❖ meeting other musicians of your own age

❖ improving your sight-reading

❖ improving your musical continuity: as the group works its way through a piece, it won't wait for you

❖ building confidence: your part might be doubled by more able players so that you can learn from them, or you may be able to help others who read music less well

INGRAM

- ❖ improving aural awareness:
  - ▪ intonation
  - ▪ rhythmic ensemble
  - ▪ control of dynamics in relation to others
- ❖ concert experience and public appreciation

You may be offered the chance to direct an ensemble yourself. Although you may feel apprehensive about this and may not have a developed conducting technique, do not turn this opportunity down as the lessons to be learned are invaluable. Here are some tips:

- ❖ listen carefully to the sound of the ensemble and decide whether it is appropriate
- ❖ concentrate on tuning, ensemble and dynamics
- ❖ mention the required style of the music without giving a history lesson
- ❖ ask specific sections (e.g. the sax section in a concert band or the altos in a choir) to perform problematic bars on their own, but avoid targeting individuals
- ❖ ask the ensemble to clap tricky rhythms
- ❖ ensure that all members of the group are listening to what you say, even if the comments do not apply directly to them
- ❖ offer some positive feedback, but qualify it with ways that the group can improve its performance
- ❖ run through the piece, or the section you have been working on, at the end of the rehearsal, and announce that everyone has made good progress

The self-directed ensemble

This includes the smaller ensembles, ranging from trios and quartets to larger groups such as a Baroque chamber orchestra or a steel band. The larger the group, the more likely it is that a director will be required.

In folk bands and jazz ensembles, which reinterpret standard popular music repertoire by use of improvisation, the players will work to a series of chords, developing a melodic motif or fitting the music to an agreed framework. Singers will need to listen carefully to recordings from the same artist if they are to imitate the style successfully. This is particularly true for soul and gospel music, where the vocal line is heavily decorated and highly expressive. Rock guitar players should also consider the nuances of a stadium solo and work out if any processors are needed to re-create the original sound.

It is important to agree on aspects of rehearsal discipline in classical ensembles, even if the work is scored. For medium-sized ensembles a leader may emerge, but he or she should take into account all voices or instruments. As there is no conductor looking at the full score, all players need to agree which melodic lines are important at any given time, so that adjustments to balance can be made. There may be moments when a general pause or a

A steel band is normally a self-directed ensemble

tempo adjustment is expected, and the group will need to develop a shared sense of the phrasing, something that can be difficult at first. Make sure that you take a soft pencil and eraser to such a session. If you are sympathetic to the technical capabilities of the instruments (in terms of maximum volume or expressive range) and the players (in terms of their level of ability), it is likely that you will find chamber music extremely enjoyable.

It can be difficult or expensive to track down music for ensembles. There are a number of websites that specialise in downloadable ensemble music, and many of these sites are free. If you are familiar with MIDI sequencers and desktop publishing scoring programs, then **www.classicalarchives.com** is one of the most comprehensive websites. Any MIDI downloads are likely to need work on display quantisation to make them readable. However, many sites provide music in PDF (which can be opened by downloading free 'acrobat reader' software) or GIF (Windows XP will open this file format). An example of such a site is **www.8notes.com**.

Original music with jazz and rock bands

A popular method of working in jazz and rock bands is to take a genuinely cooperative approach. One player may bring the initial idea to the band, and this idea is added to, enhanced or developed by various members, who make the rehearsal process into a compositional exercise. Members of the band can work together and fuse their ideas into something new. These ideas can be a series of chords, an interesting lick or riff, an unusual rhythmic device, a complete chorus or some new lyrics.

These techniques of developing an ensemble performance are often successful, as the members feel involved and work towards fulfilling their technical potential. Players are not limited by any external composer's ideas. However, it is important to remember that your music should be targeted at an audience.

Exam board assessment and grades

There is a surprising level of common agreement between the different exam boards as to what makes an outstanding performance. Taking a look at the words and phrases frequently used in the various specifications:

A-grade words: imagination; flair; persuasive; mature; committed; wholly accurate; observed all markings; completely fluent; showed understanding of the spirit of the music

C-grade words: confident; reasonable awareness; moderate technical control; competent; secure; conscientious; markings of tempo/expression/articulation/phrasing realised in some passages

E-grade words: sufficient to achieve musical intentions; adequate; modest; inconsistent; lack of variety; limited understanding; basic

Chapter 2

Composing

Composing is a coursework-assessed activity and is usually marked by an examiner rather than by your teacher. Examination boards vary in their requirements but most will expect a combination of two components:

1. A number of set tasks where you are provided with a starting point — such as a short musical opening, a series of chords or a literary stimulus — and you are expected to continue the music, flesh out the framework or illustrate the stimulus using a prescribed musical technique.

2. A free composition, where you can create you own work. However, there can be a prescribed style and or limits on duration or instrumentations.

This chapter outlines the common styles favoured by exam boards and the techniques you need to employ in order to gain high marks.

Getting started

You will need to make some decisions:

❖ What is the instrumentation?

❖ If there is a singer, what text will you set?

❖ What is the structure?

❖ What is the style? If it is tonal, in which key will it be based?

There is one guiding principle that you need to keep in mind: music is only interesting when it combines variety with unity. A tune that uses a limited number of notes has a restricted range, and use of a repetitive rhythm is likely to be boring. Such a tune may have a place in a longer composition, where contrasting ideas can set it off. However, if it is the main idea then it will fail to maintain interest. Conversely, if the tune is frantically leaping up and down, using unrelated random motifs, then the tune will not hold interest either. It is important to find a halfway house between these two extremes.

You must plan your composition. If you simply begin writing and let the ideas flow without a plan you are likely to encounter problems at a later stage in terms of structure and development. The longer a piece of music, the more important it is that it has a controlled structure. Music that consists of one tune after another can become boring to listen to. If you are composing a pop song then possible structures are set out on p. 48. Otherwise, you will have to consider a standard form, or invent one of your own. Examples include:

❖ binary: AB or AABB

❖ ternary: ABA, AABBAA or AABBA

❖ rondo: ABACADAEA etc.

❖ sonata: exposition, development and recapitulation (see p. 76)

❖ theme and variations: $AA^1A^2A^3$ etc.

❖ arched forms: ABCBA or ABCDCBA

❖ film or television music that works to a storyboard or timed framework

Most tonal music of Western Europe depends on melody. If your compositional style is more progressive the creation of thematic material is still a useful exercise. Setting words to music will at least generate a rhythm and give your music some shape. If you are composing an instrumental work then you could use a poem as a starting point and then remove the lyrics. Mozart was fond of games, billiards, dice and party tricks. Dice can be used to generate a melodic motif by ascribing notes to each number. This is better with two dice, partly to cope with the seven-note diatonic scale and also to bring in chromatic notes or different octaves. You can invent your own rules for composing using dice. Some composers have used 'chance' as their main starting point. John Cage is famous for his use of chance elements, influenced by art and Zen Buddhism.

A traditional melody derives from a key. What key are you going to choose and why? Will it be major or minor? It has already been demonstrated in Chapter 1, in the section on improvisation (pp. 22–23), that you can formulate a tune from a series of chords. You can create arpeggio patterns from the chords, filling in passing notes and then superimposing a rhythm. When choosing your chords for this method you need to remember to repeat some of them, and use the tonic and dominant chords (I and V) in the appropriate places. Alternatively you could experiment with some of the more adventurous chords set out on pp. 23–24. Here is a tune composed in this way:

Tune from chords

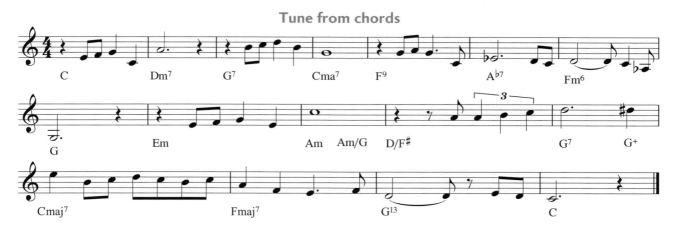

Another approach is to build up a tune from melodic fragments, perhaps only three or four notes. Beethoven made a whole movement from the opening four notes of the Fifth Symphony, and Jean Sibelius was fond of scattering musical fragments around that came together to form his main tune later in the piece. Two examples of music made from short fragments are shown below:

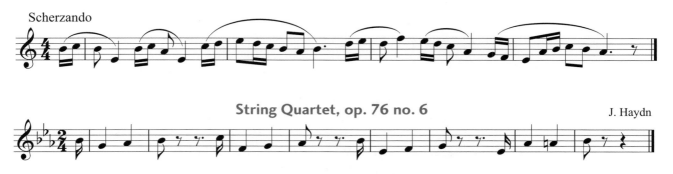

String Quartet, op. 76 no. 6 J. Haydn

You may be a good improviser and prefer to doodle at a keyboard to see what ideas you can come up with. Try using some unusual scales rather than the usual major, minor and chromatic ones. An exhaustive list of scales can be found at **www.dolmetsch.com/musictheory25.htm**. Here is a selection:

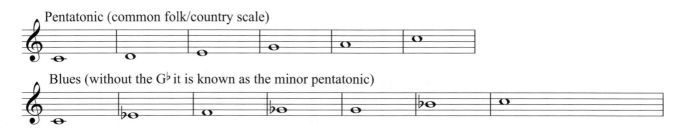

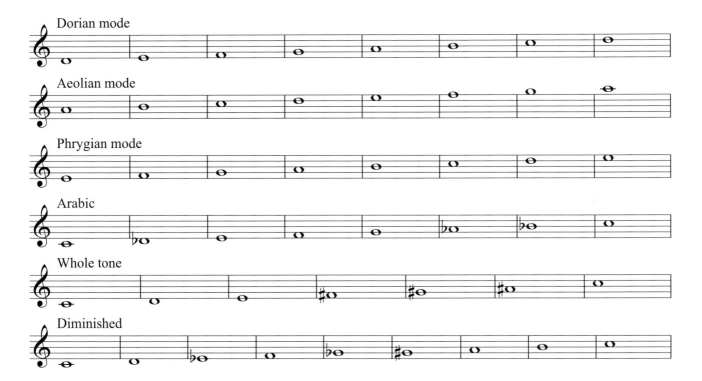

Dorian mode

Aeolian mode

Phrygian mode

Arabic

Whole tone

Diminished

If you are still seeking inspiration, look around you for an idea that can be represented in musical language. Try looking at art and architecture, literature and magazines, geography and history, or television and films for ideas. Listen to some music that excites you, have a break for a few days and then return to composing, so that you have absorbed the mood of the music but avoided copying the notes. Ideas are not copyrighted but are valuable starting points that composers through the ages have reinterpreted.

The basics of composition

Many Western styles of harmony use triads based over the notes of the major and minor scales by superimposing a 3rd and a 5th onto the root.

F major triad

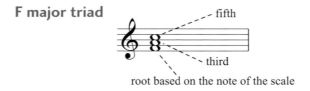

fifth

third

root based on the note of the scale

Each chord or triad has a rank order of importance; I (the triad based on the first note of the scale of the key) is the most important chord. It is used the most, as it helps the listener to work out what key the music is in, thus providing a useful reference point and sense of unity.

The rank order of the chords varies a little between different musical styles, but a common pattern is:

Primary triads			Secondary triads			
I	V	IV	II	VI	III	VII
Important ————————————————————→ Less important						

Triads in the key of C major

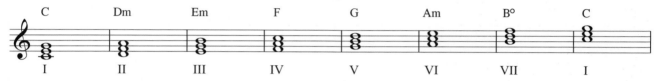

Triads in the key of A minor

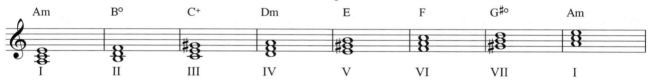

Note : C = C major, Dm = D minor, B° = B diminished, C+ = C augmented

The diminished and augmented chords (° and +) should be used sparingly, as they are difficult to handle, and the primary triads (I, IV and V) should form the basis of any harmonisation. Secondary triads give sophistication to the harmony. They can be used in certain circumstances as alternatives to the primary triads (not at cadence points – see below) as follows:

I ⟶ VI   IV ⟶ II   V ⟶ III

It is useful to sing or play through all of the parts in a vocal composition to make sure they make musical sense individually.

The notes of the triads are spread out differently according to the forces performing them. Therefore, C major could be played:

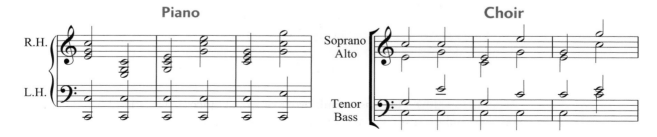

The chords above are known as **root position** chords, because the lowest note is the root note of the chord. It is possible to use chords that have the 3rd or the 5th at the bottom (often designated with a lower case letter: IVb being chord IV with the 3rd in bass). These chords are weak harmonically and are used to provide fluency and movement on weak beats. Chord VII is sometimes used as a replacement to V, but care must be taken with the movement of the parts.

Cadences are the punctuation of Western harmony. Each one uses a particular pair of chords. They are placed at the ends of phrases to give shape to the music. A description is given in Table 2.1.

Table 2.1
Description of cadences

Cadence	Chord progression	'Punctuation'	Usage
Perfect	V ⟶ I	Full stop	To conclude a melody
Imperfect	I or Ib ⟶ V II or IIb ⟶ V IV ⟶ V	Colon	To serve as a resting point in a tune, part of the way through a piece
Plagal or 'Amen'	IV ⟶ V	Full stop	Alternative, but less conclusive, ending of a melody, useful for pentatonic folk melodies that have no leading note
Interrupted	V ⟶ V	Ellipsis (…)	To twist away from an ending, leaving the music in need of resolution
Phrygian	IVb ⟶ V [in the minor key only]	Colon	A Baroque favourite for ending a slow movement in a minor key that leads into a movement in the major key

Combining tunes and unessential notes

To add a descant or to create backing vocals for a tune you must consider the relative degrees of discord that specific intervals create:

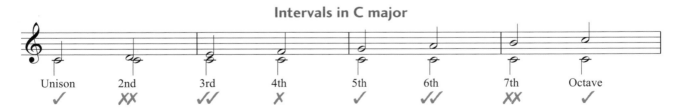

Intervals in C major

Unison	2nd	3rd	4th	5th	6th	7th	Octave
✓	✗✗	✓✓	✗	✓	✓✓	✗✗	✓

The intervals with a double tick (✓✓) underneath may be used freely when setting a descant or backing vocals, except when they contradict the harmony. A single tick means that the interval is strong but bare sounding. These should be used singly, so that they do not follow each other (for example, you should avoid consecutive 5ths). A double cross (✗✗) is a harsh discord and should not be used unless it is part of a decorative passage that uses unessential notes.

The interval of a 4th (with the single cross) is a special interval: as an interval from the major scale (perfect 4th) it creates a weak discord in older styles of music and should be treated in the same was as the 2nd and the 7th. In some modern folk and rock the 4th is acceptable if it is part of the harmony. If the upper note is sharpened, however, then the interval should not be used: this interval (an augmented 4th, also known as a tritone) is highly discordant and should only be used for special effects.

Discords can be used when the added part is more decorative. These are called **unessential notes** and common cases are displayed below, along with an example of a descant for 'O Little Town of Bethlehem'. Observe that all quaver movement is either a repeat of a note or a step (up one note or down one note).

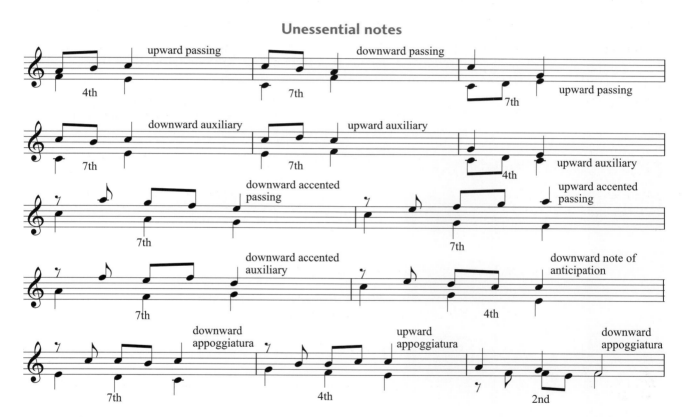

Unessential notes

O Little Town of Bethlehem

Compositional techniques

Exam boards expect students to demonstrate knowledge of the techniques used by composers in the past. Composing original work, but in the style of a particular composer, is known as **pastiche**. Sometimes exam boards require written exercises to be completed, or they provide the opening bars of a piece to be completed. This section deals with common compositional techniques. In each case a real example is given. It is much better to learn the style by studying original sources than by digesting rule books.

Bach chorales

This style is popular in music education as it crystallises many of the techniques used in harmony. It acknowledges the hierarchical relationships between chords within a key (i.e. how some chords are more important than others), and allows a degree of independent movement within the four vocal parts. At AS and A2, you may be provided with the top line of a chorale and asked to provide the lower three parts where they are missing. Here is a summary of the rules for Bach chorales:

Johann Sebastian Bach

TOPFOTO

1. There are four vocal parts, with relatively high tenor.

2. When doubling notes from triads:
   - ❖ it is best to double the root
   - ❖ it is acceptable to double the 5th
   - ❖ it is best to double the 5th in a cadential second inversion
   - ❖ it is acceptable to double the 3rd if it is a minor triad
   - ❖ it is acceptable to double the third when the bass and soprano lines are in contrary motion
   - ❖ never double the third when it is a leading note
   - ❖ always double the third in a diminished chord

3. Chords in dominant relationships produce good progressions, e.g. II–V.

4. Avoid the same harmony or the same bass note when moving from strong to weak beats.

5. Quaver passing notes and auxiliary notes are a feature.

6. Avoid consecutive 5ths and octaves.

A-Level Music Study Guide

7 Prepare discordant notes by ensuring their presence in the previous chord, then make sure that they are resolved in the next chord.

8 Sing through each part to check that it flows, concentrating on making each part sound musical, e.g. leading notes should rise.

Below is a four-part harmonisation of a tune that originally appeared in the Nuremberg hymnbook of 1569. It is derived from a secular melody by Heinrich Isaac. The melody was used by Bach several times; this version is from the *St Matthew Passion*.

Nun Ruhen Alle Wälder

J. S. Bach, BWV392

- ❖ the piece starts on chord I
- ❖ bar 1, beat 2: VIIb is a common substitute for V, except at final cadences
- ❖ bar 1, beats 3 and 4: passing notes
- ❖ bar 2, beat 1: IV^7 created by preparation of the discord in the alto
- ❖ bar 2, beat 2: inverted cadence
- ❖ bar 3, beat 1: lower auxiliary notes
- ❖ bar 3, beat 2: quaver motion in bass line (passing note) and alto line (escape note)
- ❖ bar 3, beat 4: pivot chord — III in A♭ but VI in the new key of E♭
- ❖ bar 4, beat 1: II^7 is a common preparatory chord to a cadence
- ❖ bar 4, beats 2 and 3: inverted perfect cadence in the dominant
- ❖ bar 4, beat 4: V^{7}d — one of Bach's favourite chords
- ❖ bar 5, beats 3 and 4: movement in 10ths between bass and alto idiomatic

Baroque counterpoint

This is a style that is different from polyphony, as the melody is derived purely from the harmonic progressions. This is usually indicated by figured bass, a summary of which is shown in Table 2.2 below.

5 **3** or no numbers at all	root position chord: the 3rd and 5th are added to the written bass note
6 **3** or **6**	first inversion chord: the 3rd and 6th are added to the written bass note
6 **4**	second inversion chord: the 4th and 6th are added to the written bass note
accidental under note	the accidental is applied to the 3rd of the chord
line through a number	raise the note in that position one semitone
accidental under number	apply the accidental to the 3rd of the chord and add the note given by the number to written note as bass
accidental before or after single **6**	**6** means **6–3**: apply the accidental to the 3rd
accidental before or after number	apply the accidental to the note given by the number
horizontal line after a number	the note represented by the preceding figure is to be held
7 or **8** or **9**	7th or 8th or 9th added to root position chord; this is shorthand for 7–5–3, 8–5–3 or 9–5–3
6 **5**	7th chord, first inversion; this is shorthand for 6–5–3 — the 3rd is implied
4 **3**	7th chord, second inversion; this is shorthand for 6–4–3 — the 6th is implied
4 **2**	7th chord, third inversion; this is shorthand for 6–4–2 — the 6th is implied; this chord is also called a 2 chord

Table 2.2
Figured bass

(Taken from **www.dolmetsch.com**, where there is an excellent realisation of a violin piece by Couperin that demonstrates figured bass.)

Below is an example of figured bass from Arcangelo Corelli:

Grave

Sonata for violin and basso continuo in A major

A. Corelli, Op. 5 no. 6

Points of interest:

- ❖ bar 1: arpeggio pattern in the melody
- ❖ bar 2: scalic melody
- ❖ bar 2, beat 4: sharpened D in violin part, in preparation for the modulation to V
- ❖ bar 5: transposed melody from the opening; when composing, try to identify opportunities like this to give cohesion and save work
- ❖ bar 8: contrary motion against the bass suspension on B
- ❖ bar 9: another suspension, which forms a harmonic sequence
- ❖ bar 9, beat 3: imitation in the bass of previous bar's violin melody; again, if you can use this sort of technique, it will save work
- ❖ bar 11: faster harmonic movement as the cadence approaches
- ❖ bar 12: formulaic perfect cadence in the dominant key, with a 4–3 suspension

Wolfgang Amadeus Mozart

Classical and Romantic pastiche

Composing music in the style of Mozart or Schumann requires familiarity with their works, and it will take many hours of listening to absorb their style. However, there are a number of characteristic traits that you can employ to help your music sound authentic. Classical music must sound elegant and balanced, with light textures and slow change of harmonies. Primary triads and their inversions are the staples of such music, with chromaticism reserved for special effects. The dominant 7th was

an important chord, and this chord was used frequently at cadences featuring a triple appoggiatura, as seen in the example below, where the last three quaver beats in the right hand clash with the bass.

Sonata in G

W. A. Mozart, K283, mvt. 2

Romantic music is more personal — it aims to represent the inner feelings of the composer. Consequently, it features more chromatic notes, both in the melodies and the harmonies. Note the use of chromatic notes in the following example:

Elegie

E. Grieg, from *Lyric Pieces*, op. 38

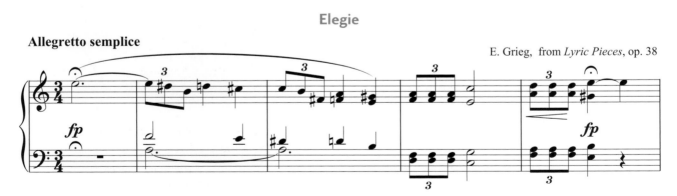

Favourites chords and progressions during this period included the minor subdominant in the major key ($\flat$IV) or 7th and 9th chords to add pathos, plus any progression that is in a mediant relationship (i.e. the roots of the chords are a 3rd apart). At this time there was a tendency towards 'showing off', either by demonstrating technical prowess with flashy bravura figurations or by exploring emotional expression. The music was often **programmatic** (being a representation of a picture, a story or a sentiment).

Home-sickness

Andante

E. Grieg, from *Lyric Pieces*, op. 57

Neo-classical style

This style of music uses classical forms such as sonata and variation, but with a modern approach to harmony and rhythm. Igor Stravinsky, Paul Hindemith, Dmitry Shostakovich, Sergey Prokofiev and Béla Bartók are usually listed as the most important composers in this area, but Darius Milhaud and his contemporary Francis Poulenc also made contributions to the genre. Some neo-classical techniques are included in the composition on p. 46.

Table 2.3
Analysis of neo-classical features

Technique	Explanation	Example
Polytonality	More than one key at a time	Bar 10, beat 4 and bar 11, beat 3 (chords made from D major and G♯ major)
Chords from 4ths	Chords derived from superimposed 4ths rather than the usual 3rds	Bars 1–5 in the right hand
Ethnic scales	Use of unusual folk scales that feature chromatic intervals	Bars 6–8 in the right hand: an old Hungarian scale
Tritone	Extensive use of the interval of the augmented 4th	Outline of motif from bars 9 and 10 (G–C♯–G in the bass line)
Added notes	Chords with additional notes in them to produce a bigger sound	Bar 6: Gm6 chord in the right hand
Ostinato	Repeated note patterns	Bars 6–8 in the left hand

A Neo-Classical Skirmish

Con moto ♩ = 135

Serialism

Serialism is a compositional technique which was explored in the early part of the twentieth century by Arnold Schoenberg and his contemporaries. Compositions had become so chromatic in the 1920s that a sense of key was no longer the binding force for the music. Schoenberg therefore came up with a scheme whereby each piece was derived from a pre-defined order of the 12 notes of the chromatic scale, which he called a **tone row**. Music is created from this row by playing each note in order. To give variety, the row can be used backwards, inverted (so, for example, a minor third would become a major sixth when inverted), or transposed. Expression is achieved through intervallic tensions, texture and dynamics. An example of a tone row is printed below, followed by the resulting composition.

Tone rows from *Suite for Piano*

O — original row

Schoenberg, op. 25

R — retrograde row (backwards)

I — inverted row

RI — retrograde inversion

Note: each of the above can be transposed to start on a different note, and the notes can be placed in any octave and/or repeated

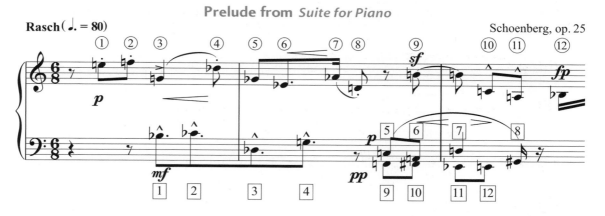

Prelude from *Suite for Piano*

Schoenberg, op. 25

Rasch (♩. = 80)

Points of interest:

❖ the circled numbers in the right hand are the original row

❖ boxed notes in the left hand are the original row transposed to start on a B♭

❖ notes 5–12 of the transposed row are used harmonically in last left hand phrase

❖ there is a high level of detail for expression and articulation

❖ there is rhythmic variety

Minimalism and aleatory music

Philip Glass

These styles are from a tradition called **Postmodernism**. Minimalism tends to be based 'around' a key rather than 'in' one and the music is often blurred by unprepared dissonance. Pieces evolve slowly over long periods of time, but for A-level work the finished product will probably need to be more compressed. Melodies and rhythms gradually change, transforming into new ones by small incremental alterations. Other features include varying textures and an avoidance of concentrated chromaticism and discords.

Minimalist composing techniques include:

❖ Additive melody, for example *Music in Similar Motion* by Philip Glass. This technique extends or reduces a

repetitive pattern by increments of the smallest rhythmic value, which thus affects the melodic content and rhythm etc.

❖ Rotation, for example Steve Reich: *Clapping Music*, *Violin Phase*. This technique involves phase shifting.

❖ Texture construction: this technique involves the ostinato fabric gradually growing more or less complex.

❖ Isorhythmic overlap, for example *Einstein on the Beach* by Philip Glass. This technique involves ostinatos of varying lengths, stated simultaneously.

❖ Rhythmic displacement, which is often the result of some of the techniques mentioned above.

An excellent website for ideas about minimalism is **www.glasspages.org**.

Aleatory music is music that has been composed using chance elements, such as notes selected by shaking dice or spinning a coin. Among the avant-garde composers of the 1970s, John Cage was famous for his experiments in this area.

Popular song

A pop song has a clearly defined structure: it usually has a chorus that contains a melodic hook with repeated words, and verses with changing words. The form is therefore often binary. It can also have an intro, an instrumental section and/or a contrasting bridge section, and an 'outro' or coda. The intro might be just two repeated chords, or a slow rhapsodic solo before the main part of the song bursts into life. The instrumental section is frequently an improvisation based on chords from another section of the song.

By definition, a pop song will have a lead vocalist, so some lyrics will be required. Inventing your own is fine (although this is unlikely to gain extra marks). If you are writing your own lyrics, you could consult a rhyming dictionary. Remember that internal rhymes are an alternative to rhymes at the end of the line (e.g. 'Are you **awake**? I'll give you a **shake**: **faking** it won't work'). You should avoid the more profound poetry, especially for upbeat music, and use repetition of lyrics in the chorus.

The song must have a clear form, which when decided upon will serve as a framework for your composition. Common formats include:

❖ verse (AABA) | chorus | verse (AABA) | chorus | bridge | chorus

❖ A | chorus | A B A | chorus | A | outro

❖ A | A | chorus | B | A | chorus | A | chorus

❖ intro | verse (AABA) | chorus | verse (AABA) | instrumental | chorus × 2

The chorus should feature any unusual melodic hook or harmonic twist that you have composed, but it should also use simpler and more direct musical language than the verse.

It isn't always necessary to produce a fully realised score. As long as your intentions are clear, and improvised sections are controlled, then examiners will give you full credit. The score below works well as a chorus hook.

Points of interest:

❖ the lead vocal features blues-style flattened 3rd notes

❖ the lead guitar contains notated licks and guided improvisation

❖ the rhythm guitar line indicates the rhythm to be strummed

❖ the bass guitar sounds an octave lower than written

❖ the drum part was auto-generated by software but edited afterwards

❖ the level of detail will satisfy the requirements of A-level examiners

Electronic and electro-acoustic music

It can be extremely stimulating to compose using electronic sounds or to create new music by processing existing acoustic sounds using a recording studio. There is a whole world of digital technology available to the young composer in the twenty-first century. If you decide that this is an area you are going to explore for your A-level composition work you should remember these guidelines:

1 The music must be recorded using the highest quality equipment possible.

2 The recording must be accompanied with detailed performance instructions if it is possible for it to be re-created in real time. A graphic score can be provided for the examiner if this is helpful, but at the very least an annotated chart should be supplied, explaining how the sounds have been produced and any processing that has been used.

3 Avoid creating compositions that depend wholly on sampled sounds of moving notes and rhythms played by someone else. Internet sites and magazine cover discs provide some exciting sound sources, but these are not your own work.

The example opposite is the first page of a screen shot from a composition created in Cubase SX. The following points would need to be made clear to an examiner if it was to be a serious submission:

❖ The time line is printed along the top (page 1 represents 30 seconds).

❖ Track 1: a recording of a choir singing a motet by Palestrina (*Sicut cervus*), which has been pitch shifted down a diminished 5th, giving it a sinister sound. It has been cut up and fade techniques have been employed so that it gradually appears and disappears (diagonal lines).

❖ Track 2: a recording of a woman's cry for help, which I produced. This has been processed using a slow panning delay.

❖ Track 3: a slow, evolving pad sound of sustained chords using the A1 (a polyphonic synthesiser that is part of the software). This uses a low pass filter that opens and closes as represented by the wavy line at the bottom of the page.

❖ Track 4: short staccato notes of random pitch with a large amount of white noise mixed in and a long decay. This uses a synthesiser/organ plug-in program that I downloaded, installed and edited.

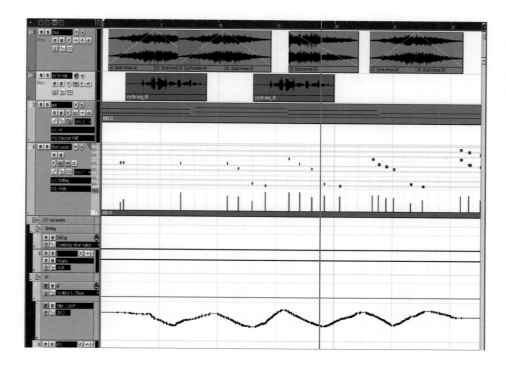

Music for the moving image or stage production

Composing music for film, television, adverts or even computer games can be an option in some specifications. Modern Hollywood film scores generally employ a post-Romantic style, with a large orchestra, sweeping melodic phrases and short motifs used to represent concepts or ideas — a technique pioneered by Wagner and known as **leitmotif**. Some famous films, however, use more modest resources. For example, *Get Carter* (1971) uses only a jazz trio, and in the original *Psycho* (1960) the composer Bernard Herrmann uses only strings. Adverts and computer game music need to be more economical in terms of duration and resources. Working with friends who study drama can provide you with ideas and will also help you to focus the music so that it fits the exact requirements of the production.

Usually you can have a free choice of musical style, but the score must demonstrate exactly how the music fits with the visual images. Where an event happens on stage or screen it is useful to make a note of it on the score. If the music corresponds exactly with a visual event it is called a **hitpoint**. The word **cue** refers to a section of music that is allocated to a section of the visuals.

Nature films (with the sound muted) are useful visual starting points. These can generate more appropriate music than a section of dialogue in a screen play (which requires the difficult task of creating unobtrusive but atmospheric music known as **underscore**). Fast-moving action scenes might require more music than you have time to create, unless you are going to use slow music to make an artistic point — the famous use of Samuel Barber's *Adagio for Strings* in the film *Apocalypse Now*, for example.

If your music is going to use traditional notation then you can employ the following formula for calculating the number of bars required in a section of the film. First of all, you must ensure that you have timed the section in seconds and made a decision about the speed you want your music to be:

$$\frac{\text{Time}}{60} \times \text{tempo} = \text{number of beats}$$

Choose your time signature and divide the number of beats by the pulse for the number of bars.

Alternatively, you can work to a storyboard of images or a cue list such as the one in Table 2.4, which is conceived for a piano quintet.

Table 2.4
Example of a cue list

Timing (seconds)	Screen images	Possible music
00.00–00.30	Fade in from black to reveal moon covered by fast-moving clouds	*Pianissimo* sustained strings building in layers; use of augmented 4ths and whole-tone scales
00.30–00.45	Camera moves swiftly down to reveal three wolves slinking though the graveyard	Strings hold long notes and piano enters, with low 4- and 5-note motifs played rapidly in octaves
00.45–01.30	Cut to teenage couple hiding behind gravestone and examining map	Strings become agitated, using repeated minor chords of quick quaver movement. The piano adds staccato 'stab' chords
01.30–02.00	Chase commences, as teenagers flee from wolves	Sudden semiquaver rushing scale patterns from all instruments, in similar motion at first but gradually turning into contrary motion and featuring high semitone trills

The music for the cue in Table 2.4 needs to blend from section to section, except the transition into the fourth (chase) section. Be aware that if every movement has a musical event attached to it, then the composition will be more suitable for cartoons. This approach is called 'micky-mousing' and it can produce music that is rather too obvious.

Music suitable for a stage production might be intended to take place between scenes (entr'acte), where a new mood can be established. Composing music for a dance production or a dance scene within a play is particularly stimulating. Make sure that you consult the choreographer first to establish whether your intentions are what the production requires. It is much more difficult to write music after the movements have been planned.

Setting words to music

Keywords:

❖ scansion: the analysis of poetry's metrical and rhythmic patterns

❖ syllabic: music that has one note per syllable of text

❖ melismatic: music that has many notes for every syllable

- trochaic: a metrical pattern of a stressed syllable followed by an unstressed syllable (long, short)
- iambic: a metrical pattern of an unstressed syllable followed by a stressed syllable (short, long)
- underlay — the alignment of syllables in the text to the musical notes

Consider the following title from the well-known jazz standard: 'What is this thing called love?' Stress each word in turn and think about the change in meaning. To communicate the intended meaning of a phrase when setting it to music you must be careful which syllables you apply the stresses to. It is not a good idea to stress less important words such as 'and' or 'the'. You must also bear in mind that syllables within words will have different degrees of emphasis. These must fit with the natural hierarchy of the time signature. This example shows the relative emphasis in common time:

In addition, you need to consider the entire musical phrase so that rhythmically and melodically important words are emphasised.

Below are two examples of word setting. The first demonstrates poor word setting, while the second example is more successful.

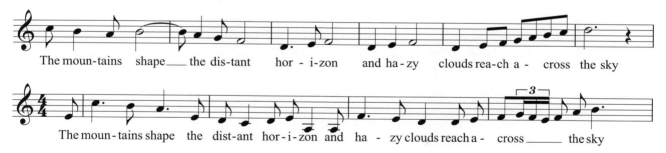

Points of interest:

- because the first word, 'The', is weak, the music should start with an anacrusis, as shown in the upbeat quaver in the second example
- 'horizon' has a stressed second syllable
- while the rising scale in the first example is a good illustration of the expansive clouds, the stress on the syllables is completely wrong
- the decoration in the last bar of the second example is effective word painting
- the six-bar phrase in the first example doesn't feel natural
- it is impossible to have fewer notes than words or syllables, as shown in the last bar of the first example
- note the convention of only beaming notes that fall on melismas

Arranging and thematic development

Exam boards often set a component that features the subject of arranging. This is where someone else's work is used as the basis for a new composition of your own. Here are a few techniques that you can use to develop a theme (in this case 'O Little Town of Bethlehem'):

❖ add an intro

❖ place the melody in the bass:

❖ place the melody in an inner part:

(Note: this is a piano texture, but it would be easier to create this with a quartet of instruments.)

❖ treat the melody contrapuntally, perhaps by using imitation:

(Note: the imitation above is not exact — the tune doesn't necessarily fit whatever note you start on. However, the slight tweak at the end of bar two is sufficiently subtle to allow the counterpoint to be effective.)

❖ break up the melody into fragments and develop these:

Allegro risoluto

(Note: this develops the second bar of the tune by descending sequence and imitation.)

❖ change key or mode:

Lento expressivo

(Note: this has been transposed to A minor and harmonised in the style of Bach.)

❖ reharmonisation

❖ change style:

Swing feel

(Note: this should be played in the style of a jazz waltz.)

When developing a theme, there are a number of techniques that can be employed:

- **sequence:** repeating fragments higher or lower, either exactly (copying the intervals) or tonally (staying in key)
- **repetition:** an obvious but valuable choice
- **inversion:** turning the intervals upside down
- **augmentation:** increasing the length of the notes proportionately, while keeping the tempo the same
- **diminution:** decreasing the length of the notes proportionately, while keeping the tempo the same
- **melodic extension:** expanding outwards by choosing an interval and gradually increasing it, for example:

Instrumentation

Table 2.5
Instrument and
vocal ranges

When writing for instruments and voices, you need to consider their capabilities and characteristics. The various ranges are set out in Table 2.5, together with some thoughts concerning their sound qualities.

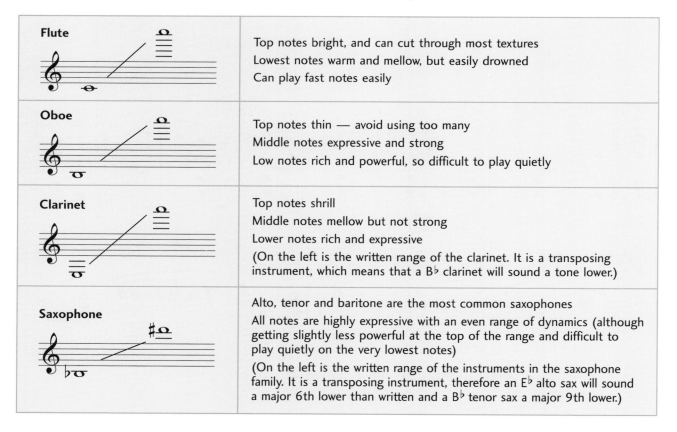

Flute	Top notes bright, and can cut through most textures Lowest notes warm and mellow, but easily drowned Can play fast notes easily
Oboe	Top notes thin — avoid using too many Middle notes expressive and strong Low notes rich and powerful, so difficult to play quietly
Clarinet	Top notes shrill Middle notes mellow but not strong Lower notes rich and expressive (On the left is the written range of the clarinet. It is a transposing instrument, which means that a B♭ clarinet will sound a tone lower.)
Saxophone	Alto, tenor and baritone are the most common saxophones All notes are highly expressive with an even range of dynamics (although getting slightly less powerful at the top of the range and difficult to play quietly on the very lowest notes) (On the left is the written range of the instruments in the saxophone family. It is a transposing instrument, therefore an E♭ alto sax will sound a major 6th lower than written and a B♭ tenor sax a major 9th lower.)

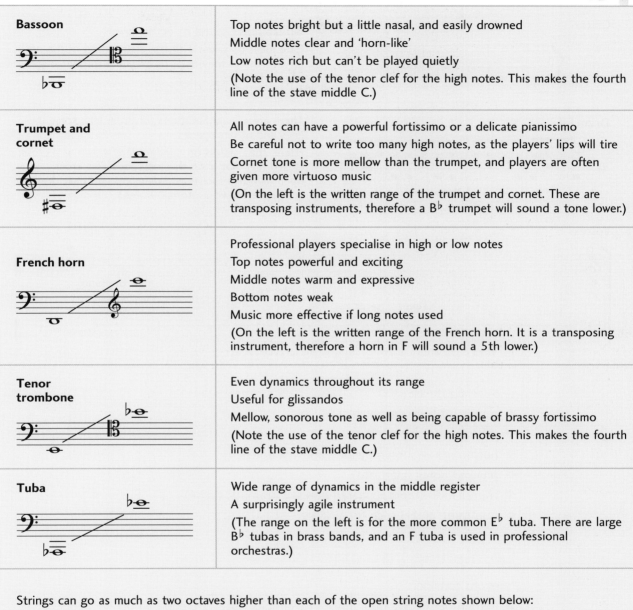

Bassoon	Top notes bright but a little nasal, and easily drowned Middle notes clear and 'horn-like' Low notes rich but can't be played quietly (Note the use of the tenor clef for the high notes. This makes the fourth line of the stave middle C.)
Trumpet and cornet	All notes can have a powerful fortissimo or a delicate pianissimo Be careful not to write too many high notes, as the players' lips will tire Cornet tone is more mellow than the trumpet, and players are often given more virtuoso music (On the left is the written range of the trumpet and cornet. These are transposing instruments, therefore a B♭ trumpet will sound a tone lower.)
French horn	Professional players specialise in high or low notes Top notes powerful and exciting Middle notes warm and expressive Bottom notes weak Music more effective if long notes used (On the left is the written range of the French horn. It is a transposing instrument, therefore a horn in F will sound a 5th lower.)
Tenor trombone	Even dynamics throughout its range Useful for glissandos Mellow, sonorous tone as well as being capable of brassy fortissimo (Note the use of the tenor clef for the high notes. This makes the fourth line of the stave middle C.)
Tuba	Wide range of dynamics in the middle register A surprisingly agile instrument (The range on the left is for the more common E♭ tuba. There are large B♭ tubas in brass bands, and an F tuba is used in professional orchestras.)

Strings can go as much as two octaves higher than each of the open string notes shown below:

Violin

Viola

Cello

Double bass/Bass guitar

(sounds an octave lower)

Note: open strings have a more direct, resonant sound than their stopped equivalents, making them stand out.

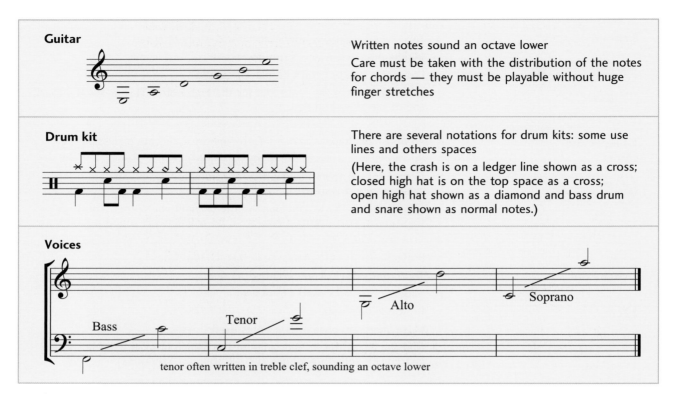

Guitar	Written notes sound an octave lower
	Care must be taken with the distribution of the notes for chords — they must be playable without huge finger stretches
Drum kit	There are several notations for drum kits: some use lines and others spaces
	(Here, the crash is on a ledger line shown as a cross; closed high hat is on the top space as a cross; open high hat shown as a diamond and bass drum and snare shown as normal notes.)
Voices	

tenor often written in treble clef, sounding an octave lower

Special effects:
- ❖ mutes for brass and strings
- ❖ glissandos and pitch bend
- ❖ harmonics — shown by an º above a note
- ❖ plucked notes (pizzicato)
- ❖ tremulando (rapid repeated notes, a dramatic cliché)
- ❖ humming and speech for singers

Combining instruments

Points to consider:
- ❖ Remember octave doubling. For example, flutes are good an octave above trumpets, brightening the sound.
- ❖ Trumpets and trombones do not need to be doubled for purposes of volume.
- ❖ Horns need to play two to a part to balance other brass.
- ❖ Never double the horn and oboe in unison, because their timbre does not blend.
- ❖ Consider natural dynamics: a high brass chord will drown a low flute solo.
- ❖ Instruments from the same family blend well.
- ❖ The different tone qualities of the woodwind are good for counterpoint

because you can pick out the different 'voices'. However, to maintain balance, use the instruments' ranges sensitively in terms of dynamics — for example, a high flute balances well with a low oboe.

❖ Divided strings (*divisi*) is good for more independent lines. Double stopping is best for harmonic blend.

❖ Give percussionists time to change instruments comfortably.

❖ Remember alternative sticks and beaters to introduce more variety with percussion instruments.

❖ Allow wind players and singers space to breathe. If a singer has to pitch a difficult note, place a reference note just before in another part.

The handling of instruments and voices is a huge subject, and space precludes too much detail in this book. To find out more look at the books by Alfred Blatter and Walter Piston listed in Further reading on p. 89. However, in a busy school music department it is possible that there may be a player of the instrument you are writing for who can try it out for you.

Music technology

A-level boards require scores of your work in order to assess your compositions. If your music is in a traditional genre there are several software packages that can help you. If you are composing in a more experimental idiom such as electronic music, it is important that other musicians can re-create your work, so you may have to devise a graphic representation of the music. This will need to be sufficiently annotated with performance directions. Your intentions need to be clear, and credit is often given for presentation. Consequently, a computer-generated score is likely to gain more marks than a handwritten one.

TOPFOTO

Computers can, however, produce some incorrect notations. Here are two examples of a printed musical theme, the first displaying errors and the second corrected.

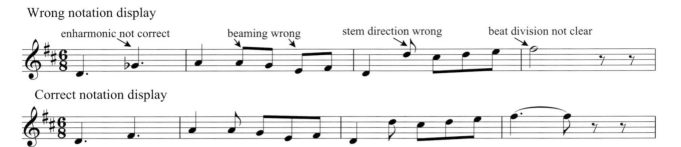

Any compositions that use electronic sounds, samples or improvisation will require a recording to be sent. The exam boards vary according to how much weight is given to the scores in such cases, but most boards use the recording as the starting point.

There are two main types of software that can help you build a composition. These divide into sequencers and scoring packages (see Table 2.6).

Table 2.6
Comparison of sequencers and scoring packages

Sequencers	Scoring packages
More useful in **real time** — entering notes on a keyboard in time to a metronome click Quick, expressive and natural, but you need good keyboard skills It is possible to use 'cycle record' to overlay ideas	More useful in **step time** — entering notes from a keyboard (or mouse) and choosing the rhythm from a menu Slow but accurate
Easy to manipulate the themes by moving them around on an 'arrange' page Any resulting score will need adjusting to avoid displaying minor human errors (quantisation) Simple to edit and apply sound processing	Working only with the score, it is more difficult to manipulate the music, but much easier to produce a readable and professional looking end result Harder to edit the expressive sound elements, but easy to represent them on the page
Simple to create audio recordings	Possible to create audio recordings, but it can be complicated
Famous brands include Cubase, Sonar and Logic	Famous brands include Sibelius and Finale
If you have the know-how you can customise the music to your own needs	Although you can customise your preferences, much is done for you automatically
Performance-orientated	Classical composing-orientated

Caution: computers can achieve things that are impossible in music, such as notes out of range or three-handed piano playing. Conversely, they make a poor imitation of the real sounds and nuances of voices and instruments, so it is always advisable to try out your work with the right forces. If you have access to sequencers and scoring packages, one way of working is to compose using a real-time sequencer, export the music as a MIDI file (a common format for all software), and import it into a scoring package. Additionally, keyboard workstations can often export MIDI files.

The finished product

Examiners will penalise scores that are not presented in the correct format, even if the composition is effective and contains interesting harmonic, melodic, rhythmic and textural ideas. Check your work against the following list:

❖ Make your intentions clear. Imagine a performer being given your score for the first time. Would he or she be able to reproduce exactly what you had in mind?

❖ Performance indications should include, where relevant, dynamics, expression, phrasing, breathing, bowing, fingering, pedalling, registration changes and special effects.

❖ Any special techniques need to be explained at the start of the piece. Explanations of drum notation are particularly important.

❖ Ensure that the instruments are presented in the correct order. For orchestral music, this is laid out in sections: woodwind, brass, percussion, singers/soloists, and strings, arranged from the highest instruments to the lowest within each section. For pop music the order is vocals, guitars, keyboards, bass and drums.

❖ Check that your enharmonic notation is correct. For example, a B♮ is the correct leading note in C minor, not a C♭. You may need to use cautionary accidentals.

❖ Check your rhythmic beaming. In 5/8 time, for example, quavers are normally grouped 3 + 2, unless there is a special rhythmic device in use.

❖ Mark the sections of your composition with double bars and rehearsal letters, where appropriate.

❖ Make sure that transposing instruments are in the right key, or make it clear on the score that all instruments are in concert pitch.

❖ If you are presenting handwritten work, check that the notes are correctly aligned vertically according to their place in the bar.

❖ Avoid unnecessary use of rests when staccato signs will suffice.

❖ Make sure the composition has an appropriate title, especially if it is programmatic, and include any visual cues if it is for stage or screen.

Exam board assessment and grades

There is a surprising amount of common agreement between the different exam boards as to what makes an outstanding composition. Taking a look at the words and phrases frequently used in the various specifications:

A-grade words: imaginative; inventive; persuasive; mature; ambitious; sophisticated; stylish; clearly realises the intentions of the composition; attention to detail — phrasing, articulation and expression marks — with any recording well balanced with tonal and dynamic contrast

C-grade words: satisfying; formulaic; competent; secure; conscientious; conventional; broadly coherent; markings of tempo/expression/articulation adequate in some sections; lacking contrast

E-grade words: just sufficient to realise the musical intentions; adequate; modest; inconsistent; lack of variety; limited understanding; basic; predictable; some technical insecurities

Ensure that your composition fits the minimum requirements for duration and substance.

Chapter 3

Appraising

Aims and strategies of listening

> The first step in any type of meaningful listening experience is the ability to hear various musical elements. Once the musical elements become familiar, participants can examine musical interrelationships, connect them to musical style and explore how they contribute to the expressive, emotional aspects of music.
>
> (M. A. Mullee, Columbia University Teachers College, dissertation abstract: development of a workshop to improve adult music listening skills)

As this quotation suggests, listening is not a separate activity from performing and composing but is integrated with all musical activities. Unless you have a clear idea of how you want music to sound when performing, you will play like an automaton, simply putting the right fingers down when particular notes appear in the score. You will not produce a musical result and will fail to communicate with your audience. In his later years, Beethoven became deaf but he could still hear his compositions 'in his head'. This is the main aim of the listening work at A-level: to develop an inner ear and then learn to apply it in order to further your musical understanding.

The inner ear puts us in the place of a listener outside ourselves. We can listen objectively to our performances and hear our compositions without having to rely on a group of instrumentalists or singers. It is important to learn to 'internalise' sounds. When we first start to read in primary school we vocalise the words, reading out loud to others or to ourselves. Gradually we develop the skill of reading in our head, at first quietly mouthing the words, later being able to scan whole lines quickly and absorb their meaning. It is much the same with musical sounds. We not only hear the sounds internally, but also bring a level of understanding to them, so that the process is useful for our studies and musicianship.

You must take every opportunity to develop and refine your inner ear. For example, when playing the clarinet in a concert band or the violin in an orchestra you are constantly presented with new music and it is easy just to play the notes without concentrating on the sound you make. It is comforting to have the security of a doubled part and the forward movement of the music to help with your sight-reading, but what sound are you making with your own instrument? How is your intonation? Are you producing a blended sound, or does the music expect you to carry a solo over the texture? Choral singing is the most effective (and the most stimulating) way of developing your inner ear. This is due in part to the fact that when singing you have to create sounds with your vocal cords after first imagining the sound in your mind.

Opportunities for listening arise every day. Think about the ring of a mobile phone or an interesting doorbell chime. Listen carefully and replay the sounds in your head. Count the sounds — how many notes are there? Focus on the sound in much the same way as you would when tuning an analogue radio. Is the rhythm even or does it involve a dotted note? Does the first interval rise or fall, and by how much?

You need a short-term musical memory in order to replay these sounds in your head. In the early days of electronic games there was a popular children's game called 'Simon'. Different coloured segments of a circle lit up and played a note. The player had to press the segment that lit up, and then progressively more and more segments lit up testing your memory. Testing isn't just diagnostic. It exercises the part of the brain responsible for short-term memory. The game is available online at **www.passionforpuzzles.com/virtualcube/simon**. Make sure you have a working soundcard and speakers or headphones. There are many more online musical games at **www.emusictheory.com**, but you will need to set the difficulty levels at 'high' to gain some benefit.

The development of the inner ear takes place gradually through involvement in musical activities. This is called **implicit listening**. Your instrumental teacher or vocal coach will ask to you to listen to the sound you produce. You are also developing your inner ear when you listen to the progress of your compositions. **Explicit listening** (work that concentrates on listening skills only) takes place in the classroom and for exams. If you seem to be struggling with listening exams, ask your teacher or the school library to invest in one of the many listening test books that are on the market. These include a CD, a variety of types of test and sometimes background information and tips. You can buy packs that are specific to your exam board. Acquiring listening skills through testing is an incremental process and cannot be achieved overnight. Discipline yourself and set an achievable target to carry out a certain number of tests per week.

Aural dictation

One common test is that of aural dictation, either rhythmic or melodic, where you have to notate music that is played to you. Here are a few approaches you can use for developing this skill. First, let's look at rhythmic dictations:

❖ It is more natural to test for rhythm when it is part of a tune rather than just a percussive or electronic sound.

❖ Try to remember the rhythm, so that you can replay it in your head.

❖ Count how many notes there are altogether.

❖ Identify the pulse, then the metre (time signature), then the rhythm in that order.

❖ Don't try to carve beautiful notes onto your paper. Just make a spot for the right number of notes and a quick line for their beams. You can add the details later:

❖ Develop an 'inner clock'. Try counting seconds in your head and then check against your watch. You need to engage with the music, not simply receive it.

❖ Use a metronome when practising. If you combine this with conducting patterns and find that you are conducting a downbeat (beat 1) when the metronome isn't sounding the first beat you know something is wrong. You will have to move the bar line.

❖ Use conducting patterns. Representing the beat by physical movement helps you place notes within the bar. It is better than just tapping your feet. If the tempo is slow and there are large numbers of notes try subdividing the beat.

❖ Use music technology to help you — perhaps a drum machine or sequencer.

❖ Check out French time names: words that when read sound like the rhythm e.g. *tafetefe* equals four semiquavers.

For pitch dictation you could:

❖ Identify the tonic. You can do this by choosing a note in the tune, singing it and then singing down the scale until you feel confident that you have reached the note that gives a sense of finality. Once the tonic is established, try to discover the starting note of the tune.

❖ Practise singing using sol-fa.

❖ Practise using **predictive vocalising**. This involves working with intervals and an instrument by:

   ▪ Playing the first note, singing it, then hearing it in your head.

   ▪ Looking at the second note, hearing it in your head, singing it, then playing it on your instrument as a check.

❖ Use a tuning fork. Invent a series of pitches that start and end on the note of your tuning fork, e.g. A–D–E–C♯–B–E–A. Sing them slowly, then check with your tuning fork that the last one is in tune.

❖ Practise defeating 'interference tones'. This is good if your exam test involves dictation with real music being played. Invent some practice exercises like the one below, where you sing the semibreve starting note, hold it in you head while the 'interference music' is played, then sing the second semibreve.

❖ Draw the contour of the melody as a graphic shape, or work out where there are steps or leaps, up or down.

❖ As with rhythmic dictation, don't put all your effort into writing the dictation beautifully. Just place dots on the right lines and spaces as the music is played, then pull the information together at the end.

Features of music

Aural awareness is not just about dictation, important though that is. At A-level you will be expected to comment on a number of other important features of the music as follows.

Texture

You will be asked to identify different types of texture, such as:

❖ **Monophonic**: a single line of melody, as in plainchant or some types of folk music. Not to be confused with monody, which refers to accompanied recitative of the early sixteenth century.

❖ **Homophonic**: all notes move with the same rhythm, creating block chords. The music can also be described as homorhythmic.

❖ **Polyphonic**: the various vocal or instrumental parts move with independent rhythms. Strict polyphony comes from the late Renaissance, when the emphasis was on the beauty of the melodic line. Counterpoint can be described as polyphonic in texture.

❖ **Heterophonic**: a melody is sounded at the same time as a variation of the same melody.

You should also listen carefully to the way that the lines combine in terms of their melodic direction. Which of the following terms would best describe this?

contrary   oblique   similar   parallel

Compositional devices

You should listen out for the compositional devices that you will have learned about when studying composition and performance. Common devices include:

❖ **Ostinato**: patterns of notes that repeat persistently through a section of the music.

❖ **Figuration**: the use of stereotyped patterns or figures.

❖ **Sequence**: patterns of notes repeated higher or lower. If you can, distinguish between tonal and real sequences. Without the bracketed F♯s the sequence below is tonal:

❖ **Pedal notes**: notes held constant as the harmony changes around them. Usually found in the bass.

❖ **Harmonic movement**: the speed of harmonic change.

❖ **Chromatic harmony**: chords not found in the key, such as the Neapolitan 6th or diminished 7th.

❖ **Suspensions**: where individual notes are held on as the harmony changes, creating discords on strong beats.

❖ **Cadences**: perfect, imperfect, plagal, interrupted, phrygian, inverted.

❖ **Modulation**:
  ◾ to the dominant (V): the bass line moves up a 5th
  ◾ to the subdominant (IV): the bass line moves up a 4th
  ◾ to the relative minor or major
  ◾ to the supertonic (II): the bass line moves up a tone

❖ **Ornamentation**.

❖ **Use of modes and unusual scales**.

❖ **Changes in tempo or time signature**.

❖ **Aspects of orchestration**, such as instrumental effects or doubling.

Historical context

It can seem a daunting task to be expected to name and date a piece of music from the Western classical tradition. If you listen to music regularly, then certain composers become relatively easy to spot: Beethoven with his tempestuous style and Bach with his introspective counterpoint. Other composers can be easily mistaken. Haydn and Mozart or Debussy and Ravel sound similar unless you know their style intimately. Exam boards make allowances for this and you will be awarded marks for being reasonably close to the right answer. Dates are always given a range in mark schemes — if the answer is 1750, for example, then you will get credit for any date between 1735 and 1765.

Be careful of jumping to conclusions. To date a piece that features a harpsichord as being composed before 1750 may seem reasonable, but the Spanish composer Manuel de Falla wrote a concerto that included one in the 1920s. You need to weigh all the evidence. Listen carefully to Stravinsky's neo-classical suite *Pulcinella*, also written in the 1920s. This is an arrangement of music by the composer Giovanni Battista Pergolesi from the 1730s. At first the music sounds as if it is simply a transcription of Pergolesi's notes, but as you listen you will be able to detect more unusual use of wind instruments and some distinctly twentieth-century harmonies. Listen to musical excerpts from a variety of perspectives.

You may be asked to name the genre of a piece. Here, it is easy to confuse opera with oratorio or symphony with symphonic poem. When exam boards set their questions they take this into account. There are, however, some indications that can help. Oratorio is more likely to employ long, worked out choruses than opera, and symphonic poems can be more literal in the presentation of their subject matter than a highly argued symphonic movement.

It may appear easier to identify genres from the twentieth century, as it is a period in musical history that is less distant. However, the greater diversity in musical styles makes the task more challenging. Even popular music and jazz styles offer changing fashions every decade. The influence of African folk traditions, American multiculturalism and technological developments all help to create a rich variety of subgenres that have their own identifiable characteristics. There are few shortcuts to help with becoming aware of these subtleties, so you need to allocate time in your day for active listening.

Using the internet

The internet has a wide variety of music that you can listen to free of charge. One site that is worth mentioning is **www.classicalarchives.com**. With the free membership this site offers, you can download from an exhaustive list of classical music saved in MIDI file format. The sonic quality of such files is dependent on the quality of the soundcard in your computer, but the music can be imported into scoring software so that you can not only view the notes but also edit them. For example, you could experiment with changing the key or the tempo. It is best to set the scoring parameters before importing the file into such software. Polyphonic music on one stave is the least successful in this format, but orchestral music with single instruments to each line works reasonably well. Vocal music does not work because the soundcard cannot reproduce the words. This site also supplies MP3 recordings, but for this you have to pay an annual subscription.

If you just want to get an idea of what a particular style or piece sounds like, you can go to a site that sells CDs, There are often free short samples of the music for you to listen to: **www.amazon.co.uk** uses this system.

The internet is also useful for researching historical information about composers, musical style and social conditions. One of the most accessible sites for this is **http://library.thinkquest.org/15413/history/music-history.htm**. Music theory and terminology, together with a historical overview, can be found at **www.dolmetsch.com**.

History and analysis

Although the study of the lives of composers and the social conditions in which they lived is helpful in gaining an understanding of musical history, A-level music specifications focus on source material. By analysing how a piece of music is put together you can gain insight into the historical trends that determine a composer's choice of compositional techniques, including how and why these techniques were employed.

Nevertheless, to put this analytical study into perspective and give your studies some human interest, a brief overview of the history of music and of European and American events is included in Table 3.1.

Table 3.1 *Brief history of music*

Musical period	Approximate dates	Composers	Musical events	World events
High Renaissance	**1500–1600**	**SACRED** **Italy:** Palestrina **Spain:** Victoria **England:** Taverner, Tallis, Byrd **Netherlands:** Lassus, de Rore **France:** Jannequin **SECULAR** **England:** Dowland, Morley, Campion, Byrd **Italy:** Monteverdi, Marenzio, Gesualdo	**The great age of polyphony, masses and motets** 1501 First book of Josquin masses 1554 First book of Palestrina masses 1575 Byrd and Tallis: Cantiones **Lute songs, madrigals, viol consorts** 1551 Susato publishes *Dansereye* 1587 Monteverdi: first book of madrigals 1588 *Musica transalpina* published 1594 Gesualdo: first book of madrigals 1597 Dowland: *The Firste Booke of Songes or Ayres*	1503 Leonardo da Vinci starts to paint the *Mona Lisa* 1509–47 Henry VIII king of England 1517 Martin Luther's 95 Theses 1534 Church of England breaks from Rome 1545–63 Council of Trent 1558–1603 Elizabeth I queen of England 1588 defeat of the Spanish Armada
Early Baroque	**1600–1650**	**Italy:** Gabrieli, Monteverdi **Germany:** Schütz **England:** Gibbons, Bull, Weelkes, Wilbye **Netherlands:** Sweelinck	**Concertato style** **The birth of opera and oratorio** 1607 Monteverdi: *Orfeo* 1611 *Parthenia* published (keyboard music by Byrd, Bull and Gibbons) 1625 Schütz: *Cantiones sacrae* 1648 Carissimi: *Jephte*	1601 Shakespeare writes *Hamlet* 1605 Gunpowder plot 1618 Thirty Years' War starts 1624–42 Cardinal Richelieu in power 1643–1715 Louis XIV king of France 1649 Charles I of England beheaded
Middle Baroque	**1650–1700**	**Italy:** Cavalli, Cesti, Corelli **Germany:** Schütz **England:** Purcell **France:** Lully, Couperin	**Development of the violin family** **Experiments with concerto grosso** **Spread of opera and the building of opera houses** 1664 Schütz: *Christmas Oratorio* 1666 the first signed Stradivarius violins appear 1681 Corelli: first book of trio sonatas 1689 Purcell: *Dido and Aeneas* 1698 Torelli: violin concertos op. 6	1660 Restoration of the monarchy in England, with Charles II taking the throne 1666 Great Fire of London 1667 Milton writes *Paradise Lost* 1685 Protestantism outlawed in France

Musical period	Approximate dates	Composers	Musical events	World events
High Baroque	**1700–1750**	**Germany:** J. S. Bach, Telemann **Italy:** Vivaldi, Scarlatti **England:** Handel **France:** Rameau	**Contrapuntal forms reach their peak with fugue** **Instrumental suite and dance forms** **Extravagant opera entertainment** 1706 Rameau: first book of clavecin pieces 1708 Bach at Weimar 1709 First piano built 1717 Bach at Cöthen 1721 Bach: Brandenburg Concertos 1724 Handel: *Julius Caesar* (opera) 1726 Vivaldi: The Four Seasons 1728 John Gay: *Beggar's Opera* 1729 Bach: *St Matthew Passion* 1735 Rameau: *Les Indes galantes* 1742 Handel: *Messiah*	1707 Act of Union: Scotland and England become one country 1712 First Industrial Revolution 1714 George I becomes king of England 1721 Robert Walpole first prime minister of Great Britain 1722–23 Russo-Persian War 1740 Frederick the Great crowned king of Prussia
Classical	**1750–1800**	**Germany:** C. P. E. Bach **Vienna:** Gluck, Haydn, Mozart, Beethoven **England:** Boyce, Clementi **Italy:** Boccherini, Cimarosa	**Piano taking over from harpsichord** **Experiments with sonata form** **Early symphonies** **Growth in public concerts** **Emergence of comic opera** 1755 Haydn's first quartets 1761 Haydn at Esterházy court 1762 Gluck: *Orfeo* 1770 Mozart's first quartets 1786 Mozart: *The Marriage of Figaro* 1791 Haydn in London 1791 Mozart: Requiem 1799 Beethoven: First Symphony	1755 First English dictionary published by Samuel Johnson 1768 James Cook discovers Australia 1775–83 American Revolution 1789–94 French Revolution 1789 George Washington elected first president of USA 1799 Napoleon becomes First Consul
Early Romantic	**1800–1830**	**Vienna:** Beethoven, Schubert **England:** Clementi, Field **Italy:** Rossini, Bellini **Germany:** Weber **France:** Berlioz, Cherubini	**Musical soirées** **Chamber music** **Overtures as independent forms** **Symphonies and concertos** **Comic opera** **Lieder** 1807 Beethoven: Fifth Symphony 1815 Invention of the metronome 1816 Rossini: *The Barber of Seville* 1821 Weber: *Der Freischütz* 1826 Schubert: *Der Winterreise* 1830 Berlioz: *Symphonie Fantastique*	1805 Battle of Trafalgar 1810 Sir Walter Scott writes *The Lady of the Lake* 1813 Napoleon abdicates 1813 Jane Austen: *Pride and Prejudice* 1815 Battle of Waterloo 1829 Balzac: *La Comédie humaine*

Musical period	Approximate dates	Composers	Musical events	World events
Romantic	**1830–70**	**Germany/Austria:** Schumann, Mendelssohn, Wagner **Italy:** Donizetti, Verdi **Poland/France:** Chopin, Gounod, Offenbach **Hungary:** Liszt **Norway:** Grieg	**Influence of literature and the arts** **Virtuoso music (especially piano)** **Music drama** **Early nationalistic ideals** 1832 Mendelssohn: first volume of *Songs without Words* (piano) 1832 Chopin: études and mazurkas 1834 Schumann founds music journal *Neue Zeitschrift für Musik* 1838 Schumann: *Kinderscenen* and *Kreisleriana* c. 1840 invention of the saxophone 1842 Verdi: *Nabucco* 1843 Wagner: *The Flying Dutchman* 1859 Wagner: *Tristan and Isolde* 1871 Grieg: first set of *Lyric Pieces* for piano	1837 Queen Victoria crowned 1848 Marx and Engels publish *Communist Manifesto* 1849 Dickens: *David Copperfield* 1859 Darwin: *The Origin of Species* 1861–65 American Civil War 1864 Carroll: *Alice in Wonderland* 1865–69 Tolstoy: *War and Peace*
Late Romantic	**1870–1900**	**Vienna:** Brahms, R. Strauss, J. Strauss (ii), Bruckner, Mahler **Russia:** Borodin, Rimsky-Korsakov, Musorgsky, Tchaikovsky	**Symphony and symphonic poem** **Nationalism** **Music becoming more chromatic** **Orchestra expands in size** 1874 J. Strauss: *Die Fledermaus* 1874 Musorgsky: *Pictures from an Exhibition* 1874 Smetana: *Má vlast* 1876 Wagner: first complete performance of 'The Ring' cycle of operas 1877 Brahms: Symphony no. 1 1878 Brahms: Symphony no. 2 1885 Gilbert and Sullivan: *The Mikado* 1887 Verdi: *Otello* 1888 Satie: *Gymnopédies* 1888 Tchaikovsky: Symphony no. 5 1888 Strauss: *Don Juan* 1889 Mahler: Symphony no. 1 1894 Dvořák: *New World Symphony* 1896 Puccini: *La bohème*	1880–1902 Boer Wars 1889 Paris World's Fair 1894 Kipling: *The Jungle Book*

Musical period	Approximate dates	Composers	Musical events	World events
Impressionism	1894–1920	**France:** Debussy, Ravel, Fauré, Satie **England:** Delius	**Start of the break-up of the tonal system** **Parallelism and whole-tone scales** 1894 Debussy: *Prélude à l'après-midi d'un faune* 1905 Debussy: *La mer* 1912 Ravel: *Daphnis et Chloé*	1902 Monet: *Waterloo Bridge* 1912 Titanic sunk 1914–18 First World War
Post Romantic	1900–1950	**England:** Holst, Elgar, Vaughan Williams **Finland:** Sibelius **Russia:** Rachmaninoff **America:** Copland	**Large forces producing emotional content** **Nationalistic elements** 1900 Elgar: *The Dream of Gerontius* 1901 Rachmaninoff: Piano Concerto no. 2 1915 Sibelius Symphony no. 5 1943 Vaughan Williams: Symphony no. 5	1922 BBC first radio broadcasts 1924 First Labour government in the UK 1926 Votes for women 1926 British general strike 1929 Wall Street crash 1932 BBC first television broadcasts 1939–45 Second World War
Modern	1900–present	**Vienna:** Schoenberg, Webern, Berg **Germany:** Weill, Hindemith **England:** Britten, Tippett **Russia:** Stravinsky, Shostakovitch. Prokofiev **America:** Bernstein, Ives, Piston **Hungary:** Kodály, Bartók **France:** Messiaen	**Breakdown of tonality: serialism, chromaticism and atonality** **Neo-classicism** **Ethnic scale** 1911 Bartók: *Allegro barbaro* (piano) 1913 Stravinsky: *The Rite of Spring* 1913 Webern: *Six Orchestral Pieces* 1916–17 Prokofiev: Classical Symphony 1926 Kodály: *Háry János* 1928 Weill: *The Threepenny Opera* 1930 Stravinsky: *Symphony of Psalms* 1935 Berg: Violin Concerto 1937 Shostakovich: Fifth Symphony 1939 Bartók Sixth String Quartet 1945 Britten: *Peter Grimes*	1953 Elizabeth II crowned 1956 Suez Crisis 1957 Festival of Britain 1958 Khrushchev becomes premier of USSR 1963 Assassination of President Kennedy 1965 USA sends troops to Vietnam 1969 First men on the moon 1976 First Apple home computers 1979 Margaret Thatcher becomes prime minister 1981 First PC home computers 1991 Collapse of the Soviet Union

Musical period	Approximate dates	Composers	Musical events	World events (cont.)
Experimental music and the avant-garde	**1930–present**	**Italy:** Berio **Germany:** Henze **France:** Boulez, Varèse **England:** Birtwistle, Nyman, Tavener **USA:** Cage, Reich, Glass **Poland:** Penderecki, Lutoslawski	**Electronic music** **Minimalism** **Influence of popular music/jazz** 1931 Varèse: *Ionisation* 1948 Cage: *Sonatas and Interludes* for prepared piano 1953 Stockhausen: *Kontra-Punkte* 1954 Boulez: *Le marteau sans maître* 1966: Penderecki: *St Luke Passion* 1968 Berio: *Sinfonia* 1976 Glass: *Einstein on the Beach*	1993 Growth in use of the internet 1997 Death of Princess Diana 2001 Terrorist attacks in New York and Washington 2003 Iraq war 2004 Asian tsunami
Popular music and jazz	**1900–present**	Note: composers and performers often the same 1899 Scott Joplin: *Maple Leaf Rag* 1905 Jelly Roll Morton: *Jelly Roll Blues* 1923 Bessie Smith records *Downhearted Blues* 1932 Duke Ellington: *It don't mean a thing* 1933 Hammond organ developed 1937 Glenn Miller Band has its debut in New York 1942 Bing Crosby releases *White Christmas* 1956 Elvis Presley's first album 1957 Bernstein: *West Side Story* 1959 Miles Davis: *Kind of Blue* 1963 The Beatles and the Rolling Stones' first albums 1964 Robert Moog's analogue synthesisers 1975 Punk rock in the UK 1982 Michael Jackson: *Thriller* 1983 Yamaha DX7 digital synthesiser 1985 Madonna: The Virgin Tour 1988 CDs outsell vinyl 1996 Virgin puts 24-hour radio on the internet 1999 Napster online music started 2001 The iPod is launched by Apple 2003 www.myspace.com allows bands to upload their music	

A useful starting point when looking at the history of a piece is to discover when it was written and what was going on in the world at that time. This can provide insights into why the piece was written and why it used particular conventions of form, musical language and instrumentation. Further information about historical context is given in Chapter 1.

When you study a piece of music, you need to work out how it is put together so that you can learn from the composer's techniques and apply them to your own performing, composing and listening. The skills of musical analysis needed for this process are common to all A-level specifications.

Before beginning any musical analysis it is a good idea to listen carefully to recorded performances of the piece so that you are familiar with the sounds and forward motion of the music. Have paper and a pencil handy to jot down your first impressions:

- ❖ Did you notice any important sectional repeats? Was there a clear formal structure?

- ❖ Where were the main points of rest, or cadence points?

- ❖ Was the musical language mainly tonal, i.e. did it have a sense of key?

- ❖ Were there any identifiable motifs or memorable fragments of melody?

- ❖ Were there any rhythmic features or patterns?

- ❖ Was the instrumentation unusual? If so, why?

- ❖ What was the predominant texture? Block chords? Counterpoint?

- ❖ Was there a prevailing emotional mood?

Once you have thoroughly internalised the sounds you can look more closely at the score without the music playing. Sectional repeats should be easy to identify. Why are they there? Is the repeat an expected part of the form? For example, dances of the Baroque period are normally in binary form, in which each half is repeated.

Musical analysis at A-level involves the careful study of musical scores combined with an aural awareness of the music itself. You must discover what makes the music work in terms of structure. This will be defined by thematic material and its development, harmony, melody, texture and rhythm.

The most important form to emerge in the history of Western Europe was sonata form. It developed during the mid-eighteenth century and was used for symphonies, concertos and many first movements in chamber music. This was a complex form that depended on relationships of key for its effectiveness. A summary is set out in Table 3.2.

Introduction (optional)	Exposition				Development	Recapitulation			
	First subject (group)	Transition	Second subject (group)	Codetta	Themes chopped up, extended, treated in sequence, used contrapuntally, sent through different keys, inverted, combined, diminished or augmented	First subject (group)	Transition	Second subject (group)	Coda
(V or I)	I	Changing key	V (or relative major)	V	Various keys	I	Changing key	I	I

Table 3.2
The structure of sonata form

Note: the introduction is often not present, particularly in early Classical works. If the movement is in a minor key, the second subject is normally in the relative major rather than the dominant. The transition sections usually contain episodic music that modulates. In the recapitulation, the modulation ends up staying in the tonic so that the work finishes in the home key. Subject groups often contain more than one theme. As time went on, the development section and the codetta/coda tended to get longer. The exposition is usually repeated but the development and recapitulation are not. In concertos, the repeat of the exposition features the soloist and a cadenza is usually inserted before the coda.

Earlier, during the Baroque period, composers often used fugue form for serious works. This important form developed a short motif called a **subject** through various compositional devices, giving the music the sense of forward motion its literal translation implies ('fugue' comes from the word 'flight' and developed from the earlier instrumental form of ricercare, meaning 'to search for' in Italian). Fugue form is found throughout the keyboard works of Handel and Bach. Sometimes it is used for choral and orchestral music, although often the simplified version (fugato) of this complex essay in counterpoint is used instead. The form consists of an **exposition** (where the subject enters in each of the voices, one after another), followed by **episodes** (where the music modulates to a new key). New entries of the subject in the new key follow this, leading to another episode that takes the music onwards to yet another key. Eventually the music concludes by returning to the key in which it began.

J. S. Bach is considered to be the greatest composer of fugues. His collection known as *The Art of Fugue* set out a comprehensive variety of approaches of treating a fugue subject. Bach's 48 Preludes and Fugues for clavichord are famous for their demonstration of the tuning system known as 'equal temperament', and there are two fugues for every possible key.

An imaginary opening exposition of a fugue is represented graphically below:

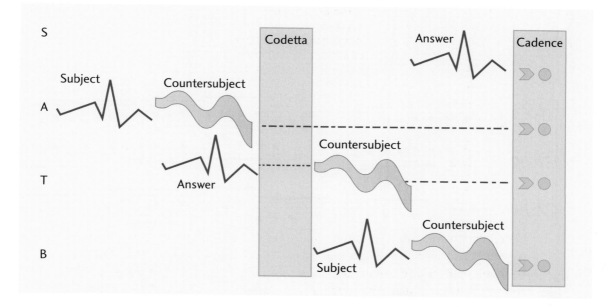

This fugue has four voices, entering in the order of alto (A), tenor (T), bass (B), soprano (S). It has a short, inserted section after the tenor entry known as a **codetta**, which is there principally to build tension by delaying the expected bass entry of the subject. The dotted lines represent 'fill in' music that is less significant thematically.

Fugue form persisted into the Classical and Romantic periods but by then was viewed as old-fashioned. A famous example of anachronistic usage is found in Brahms's Academic Festival Overture.

Analysis of specific works

It is impossible to analyse every kind of piece that might be set by an examination board. The following works have been chosen for their different styles to demonstrate the techniques of musical analysis. You should practise these techniques on other pieces and ask your teacher if your results are correct. Often you are allowed to take unmarked scores into your exam, and if you become proficient at dissecting a piece of music you will be able to use this skill under exam conditions. In addition, the ability to hear scores in your head will be invaluable in an exam.

Below is a short instrumental movement used as the opening to Bach's funeral cantata *Gottes Zeit ist die allerbeste Zeit*, BWV106. It is used here to demonstrate some of the aspects of harmony that you can take into account when carrying out an analysis, remembering the context for which the music was originally composed.

Sonatina

from *Gottes Zeit ist die allerbeste Zeit*

J. S. Bach, BWV106

A-Level Music Study Guide

Harmonic analysis by bar

I	IV7	IIb	V7d Ib II VII	I IV7 V7 V	I VII	I	I7

Eb major   tonic pedal - dom. 7th

IV	IIb	V7d Ib VI			V	V7d
			VII V I	*II#7b* V	*I*	

Bb minor

Ib I VI *VI7d*	Ib I *VI VI7*		VI VII V7	I	I7b I7
	V V7	Ib I IV V4-3	I		dom. 7th

F minor

I	*IIb II7*	V V7d Ib IV	Ic IVb vIIV V	I	I7	IV	V7 I

dom. 7th   dom. 7th

tonic pedal -

(Note: standard letters have been used to denote chord inversions. For example, Ib is the same as I $^6_3$. Chords in italics have a raised 3rd).

Listening carefully to the music in conjunction with the bar-by-bar analysis of the harmony set out above allows us to draw the following conclusions:

❖ The music is divided into two halves by a perfect cadence in the dominant (Bb major) in bars 9–10.

❖ The use of the tonic pedal in the continuo part helps to maintain the sense of calm that is required, providing a solid harmonic structure.

❖ The second half of the piece moves a little further away tonally. It reaches a cadence in the supertonic (F minor) in bars 12–13 and uses harmonic sequence to create a sense of gentle motion (bars 10–12 and 13–15).

❖ The harmony changes while the melody remains constant in bars 16–17.

❖ Third inversion 7th chords appear more than is usual in standard harmony. Bach liked these types of chords and they are often generated by a need for scalic movement in the bass.

❖ The choice of the key of Eb major helps the subdued tone (note the Baroque convention of a missing flat in the key signature).

Additional thoughts concerning the appropriateness of the music for the introduction to a funeral cantata include:

❖ The instrumentation: low flutes or recorders and the rich sound of viola da gambas together with the organ make a warm and comforting sound.

❖ The prominent feature of the falling sixths in the recorder lines is a musical convention for a sigh, giving a resigned sadness to the movement.

❖ The interplay between the two recorders is designed to reinforce the most important parts of the melody, which could get lost with these quiet sounding instruments. The sections that weave the two recorder parts together (such as bars 7–8) seem to be describing a personal and intimate relationship.

❖ The slow pulsing quaver movement is dignified and ceremonial.

Another piece of music in the same key, but from a very different time (1933) is printed below. The analysis that follows concentrates on the melody line.

Smoke Gets In Your Eyes

Otto Harbach

Jerome Kern

- ❖ The song is constructed in the standard 32-bar format, comprising four lots of eight-bar phrases.

- ❖ The first phrase rises to a climax on F after the held E♭. It then reverses this build-up with a gradual move down to the lower register.

- ❖ The first four bars confine the melodic movement within each bar to one or two notes up or down, while in the second four bars the melodic movement is more disjunct.

- ❖ The middle eight bars begin on a D♯, which is the enharmonic equivalent of E♭.

- ❖ The middle eight bars suggest partial rhythmic retrograde in the melodic line, with the quaver movement present at the start of each bar.

It is worth bearing in mind the social context of the song: smoking in the 1930s was a fashionable pastime without the associated health concerns of today. This song was a favourite tune at that time and it has been arranged and orchestrated by many bands.

The following piece of Romantic piano music demonstrates variety of texture:

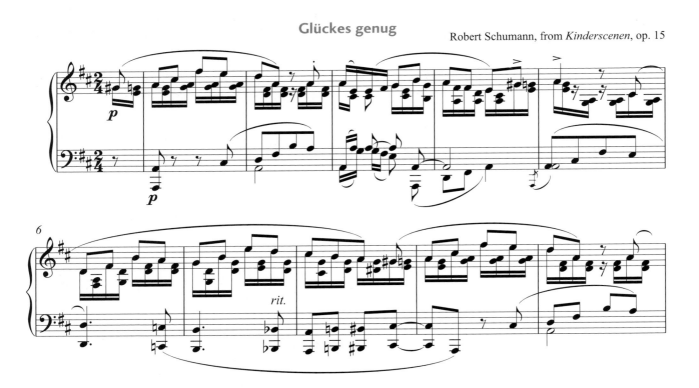

Glückes genug

Robert Schumann, from *Kinderscenen*, op. 15

- ❖ The melody begins in the right hand with a seven-note rising and falling phrase. The accompaniment to this melody consists of off-beat semi-quavers derived from the harmony. Before the phrase concludes an echo of it dovetails in the left hand.

❖ The second phrase is also in the right hand and overlaps the left-hand echo of the first phrase with a partially inverted answer. There is a rising arpeggio in D major in the bass part, which also features some rhythmic imitation.

❖ The opening music seems to return with the accented anacrusis at the end of bar 4, but in fact Schumann gives the theme to the left hand, with the right hand producing a copy of the left-hand echo from bar 2. This time, however, the theme is extended by melodic sequence, while the bass harmonies descend chromatically.

❖ The ritenuto that starts in bar 7 holds the music back to relish the expanded texture that moves in contrary motion. A thematic repeat begins in bar 9. At this point Schumann produces a four-part texture that maintains a highly pianistic style and flows forward with confidence.

The following piece of modern piano music demonstrates variety of rhythm:

Sonata for pianoforte

Béla Bartók SZ80 mvt 3

❖ The constant quaver rhythm (*perpetuum mobile*) and fast tempo marking creates an exciting forward motion.

❖ The metric alternation (3/8 into 2/4 and other metres) pushes the music forwards and gives it a bouncing, dance-like quality.

❖ The 1/4 metre in bar 4 sounds short — a 2/4 bar is expected here. This has the effect of pushing the music forward on the return of the theme in bar 5.

❖ The theme is repeated from bars 5–8, but the second phrase moves downwards and bar 8 is now extended to 2/4 metre to give a little more finality.

❖ The stabbing added 2nd chords on off-beats punctuate the music.

❖ The opening eight bars are repeated from bar 9 at a higher octave.

❖ The music settles down to what appears to be a lilting rhythmic accompaniment in bars 17–19, but increases in volume towards an accent that leads into the new section. Here we are presented with a new theme, derived from the original, inverted and placed in the bass. The 6/8 time signature gives a more settled feel for a short time, but the music then continues to move forwards relentlessly.

Exam questions

Remember to read the question carefully. It is common for students to revise frantically, memorising notes or essays they have produced during the year, and then to reproduce these essays in the exam answer booklet simply because one word they recognise is present in the question. You must ensure that you avoid this approach.

Imagine this is the question you are presented with in an exam, assuming you have made a study of the orchestral score in question:

Does Debussy's use of instruments and textures realise the aims of the Impressionist movement in his tone poem *Prélude à l'après-midi d'un faune*?

First, you will need some sort of introduction to your essay, explaining the way you intend to tackle the question. There are a number of points that need to be addressed, which are implicit in the question, and you could set these out:

❖ the basic aims of the Impressionist movement

❖ a brief summary of the orchestral forces that Debussy used

❖ the clarity of the texture

Next, you can move on to the main part of the essay. You will need to show how the orchestra is used to create an Impressionistic representation of the original poem by Stéphane Mallarmé, particularly through Debussy's orchestration and control of texture. Highlight any unusual combinations of instruments and transparent textures (for example, you could refer to the way the low flute solo isn't drowned by the accompaniment when it returns for a second time).

Any statements you make about the Impressionist style need to be backed up with hard evidence from the score. Relate all you comments to *Prélude à l'après-midi d'un faune*, giving specific references and bar numbers, even if you have studied other French music in depth. Avoid a lengthy discussion of tone poems.

Finally, you will need a short concluding paragraph that states your view (if it is your view) that this early work by Debussy does indeed realise the Impressionist aims through orchestration and texture. Do not be tempted to introduce anything new in your conclusion, such as Debussy's harmony. There will be no marks allocated to this and it will spoil the flow of your argument.

Here is another possible question:

Compare and contrast the instrumental techniques and musical styles used by Louis Armstrong in *West End Blues* with those of Miles Davis in the opening of *Four*.

First, it is important to remember that **compare** refers to similarities, whereas **contrast** refers to differences. You should begin your answer with a short introduction. This could include how both Louis Armstrong and Miles Davis are known as trumpet players who were highly original and influential, shaping the history of jazz for many years. The introduction could also give some background history to put the music into context and could refer briefly to the other members of the ensembles. However, the focus of this particular question is on trumpet playing, so the main body of your answer should focus on this.

You could begin your second paragraph with a brief description of the similarities between the two works. Armstrong and Davis were both daring, experimental players (back this point up with evidence, such as the range of notes used or technical tricks like pitch bend in specific bars). In these examples, both trumpeters play a lead role in the ensemble and both use improvisation derived from the chord progressions.

The next paragraph would then need to focus on the differences between the pieces. This could include how Armstrong's improvisations use scales and arpeggios derived from a relatively simple harmonic language with a blues orientation, whereas Davis's melodies are more chromatic and linear. In addition, Davis uses a greater variety of tone colours and range of notes and develops the melodies over a greater number of bars.

Most of the points above have addressed the question of instrumental techniques; you could draw the essay to a conclusion with reference to the styles of New Orleans and Bebop. However, you need to remember to be specific in your answers. It is important that you do not put forward opinions about which style you like the best. Musical history at A-level is an objective exercise.

These two questions were based on music published in *The New Anthology of Music* (ed. Julia Winterson, 2000, Peters Edition), for the Edexcel examination board. OCR often invites candidates to comment on musical examples that are not necessarily specified. The question on p. 86 is taken from one of its specimen papers:

Choose any one work by Purcell to illustrate his effective setting of the English language.

To answer this you should choose just one specific work to draw your illustrations from, as this is what the question asks you to do. Avoid referring to a range of pieces. In addition, choose music that will help you answer the question comprehensively. Expressive recitative or arioso will give you more opportunities to discuss word setting than choruses or even duets. If you choose the famous aria at the end of *Dido and Aeneas* ('When I am Laid in Earth') it would be useful to include the preceding recitative, with its sinking pitches representing fateful resignation.

Make sure you have all the technical terms at your fingertips. Are you familiar with the various poetic devices of scansion? Do you have a thorough understanding of Baroque harmony and figured bass? Do you understand the individual style that Purcell employs when writing his melodic lines, in terms of both rhythms and intervallic inflections?

Appendices

Key signatures

The rhythm pyramid

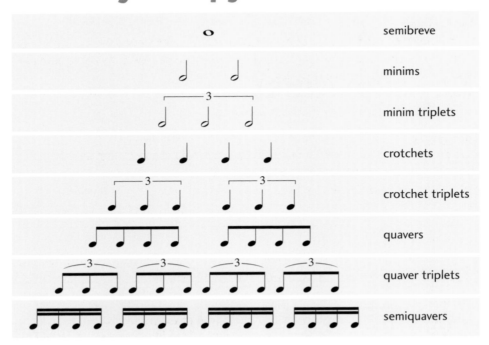

o	semibreve
	minims
	minim triplets
	crotchets
	crotchet triplets
	quavers
	quaver triplets
	semiquavers

Rests

Breve (8 crotchet beats)   Semibreve (4)   Minim (2)

Crotchet (1)   Quaver ($\frac{1}{2}$)   Semiquaver ($\frac{1}{4}$)   Demisemiquaver ($\frac{1}{8}$)

Clefs

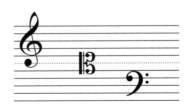

Further reading

Performing

A Performer's Guide to Music of the Baroque/Classical/Romantic Period (various authors — see **www.abrsmpublishing.com/publications** for details), ABRSM — each of the three books includes a CD.

Brown, H. M. and Sadie, S. (ed.) (1989) *Performance Practice: Music after 1600*, Macmillan — detailed and comprehensive.

Composing

Blatter, A. (1997) *Instrumentation and Orchestration* (2nd edn), Schirmer.

Butterworth, A. (1999) *Harmony in Practice*, ABRSM.

Cole, B. (1996) *The Composer's Handbook*, Schott — clear and easy to use.

Felts, R. (2002) *Reharmonization Techniques*, Berklee Press — mostly jazz-orientated.

Piston, W. (1955) *Orchestration*, Gollancz.

Stewart, D. (2000) *Inside the Music: The Musician's Guide to Composition, Improvisation and the Mechanics of Music*, Backbeat UK.

Listening

Bowman, D. (1995) *Aural Matters*, Schott — lots of examples on CD.

Karpinski, G. S. (2000) *Aural Skills Acquisition: The Development of Listening, Reading, and Performing Skills in College-Level Musicians*, OUP.

Kernfeld, B. (1995) *What to Listen for in Jazz*, Yale — comes with a CD and in-depth analysis.

History

Abraham, G. (1979) *The Concise Oxford History of Music*, OUP — history through genres.

Bowman, D. (1993) *Analysis Matters*, Schott — advice from a former chief examiner.

Bricheno, T., Nickol, P. and Winterson, J. (2003) *Pop Music: The Text Book*, Peters — an excellent overview of pop.

Cole, W. (1997) *The Form of Music*, ABRSM.

Cooke, D. (1978) *The Language of Music*, OUP — detailed analysis on melodic shape.

Grout, D. J. (2005) *A History of Western Music*, W. W. Norton & Co Ltd — history through composers.

Rosen, C. (2005) *The Classical Style: Haydn, Mozart and Beethoven*, Faber and Faber.

Sadie, S. and Latham, A. (1996) *The Cambridge Music Guide*, Cambridge University Press — simple but comprehensive.

Sutro, D. (1998) *Jazz for Dummies*, IDG.